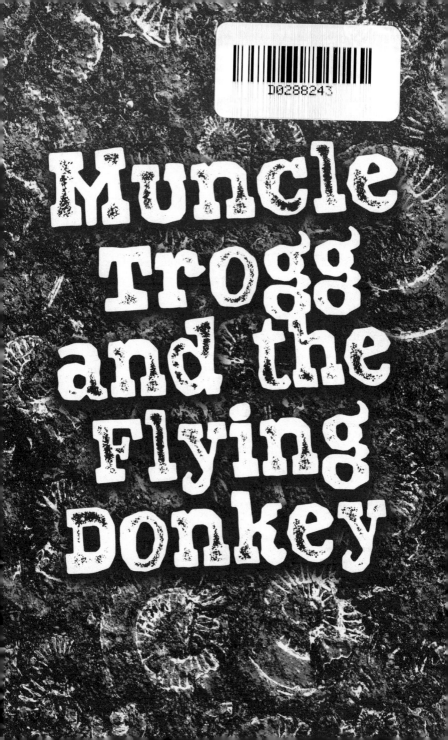

Muncle Trogg and the Flying Donkey

From The Chicken House

Muncle has been busy becoming a star since his first book became a bit of a bestseller. He's been translated into lots of different languages, and has even taken a trip to Hollywood (Emily went too, of course)!

Thankfully he's back in Mount Grumble now, as his friends and family really need his advice ...

I love Muncle's stories. Janet Foxley is writing future classics and this small publisher fellow (that's me) thinks they're wonderful!

Barry Cunningham
Publisher

2 Palmer Street, Frome, Somerset BA11 1DS
www.doublecluck.com.

Janet Foxley

Illustrated by Steve Wells

Muncle Trogg and the Flying Donkey

(He's a giant, but a tiny one)

Dedication
For Donald, Rachel and Sebastian,
with love and gratitude

Text © Janet Foxley 2012
Illustrations © Steve Wells 2012

First published in Great Britain in 2012
The Chicken House
2 Palmer Street
Frome, Somerset BA11 1DS
United Kingdom
www.doublecluck.com

Cover, illustration, typesetting and interior design by Steve Wells
Printed and bound in Great Britain by CPI Group (UK) Ltd, Croydon CR0 4YY

The paper used in this Chicken House book is made from wood grown in sustainable forests.

1 3 5 7 9 10 8 6 4 2

British Library Cataloguing in Publication data available.

ISBN 978-1-906427-95-5

DANGER
LOW-
FLYING
Giants
AHEAD!

Please wipe your feet
before you come in

MUNCLE
TROGG:
World's tiniest
giant

GRITT
TROGG:
Muncle's giant
little brother

PA TROGG:
Champion cow
hunter

Meet Muncle and his family

MA TROGG:
Cooker of
disgusting fungus-
based stews

FLUBB TROGG:
Muncle's
baby sister

If you're sitting
comfortably, then
we'll begin...

Pa is outwitted by cows.

Chapter One

'Don't drop me, Gritt!' shrieked Muncle, bouncing on his younger brother's huge shoulders.

'Sorry,' puffed Gritt, 'but Pa's at the Smalling farm already. I don't want to miss seeing him catch an ox. It'll be so exciting!'

Muncle clung to Gritt's hair as he charged down the mountain, scattering sheep.

It was their first hunting trip. Until the Great Smalling Battle – the first one for centuries – only hunters like Pa were allowed out of Mount Grumble, and they had to creep out at night. But now that they'd made the Smallings run away, King Thortless the Thirteenth had said everyone could go out whenever they liked, even in broad daylight.

Pa was waiting for them at the bottom of Mount

Grumble, next to the Smalling fields. On the other side of a thin metal fence were some sleepy-looking black-and-white animals. They watched the three giants curiously. The fields were covered with dark-brown puddles.

Gritt dumped Muncle on the ground.

'Thanks,' said Muncle. For once it had been useful to have a younger brother who was the strongest seven-year-old in Mount Grumble. It'd have taken him donkey's years to get here on his own.

'Are these the oxen?' Gritt whispered in awe.

'Cows,' said Pa. 'Same thing, just a bit smaller.'

'They're still a lot bigger than sheep,' said Muncle.

'But not as big as me.' Pa puffed out his chest. 'And they're really, really slow. I'll catch one in no time.'

He leapt over the metal fence.

The cows began to back away.

'Mind you don't touch the fences, boys,' said Pa, unfolding his hunting net. 'The Smallings put spells on them.'

'Spells?' said Muncle. 'What makes you think that?'

'I bumped into one once and the magic ran through me like a shiver. You'd better go round by the gate, Muncle. The fence is too high for you. Gritt, you come with me. And mind the splats.'

'The what?' Gritt stepped carefully over the fence.

'Splats.' Pa pointed to the dark-brown puddles. 'It's the proper name for cow-plops. Now, boys, this is how you hunt a cow. You chase it, then throw the net over it, and wrestle it to the ground. Watch and learn.'

Pa ran after the cows.

Gritt ran after Pa.

The cows ran away. They weren't that slow after all.

Muncle sighed. This was going to take a long time.

He made his way towards the gate, thinking. How could such a thin fence keep in all those big cows? His Smalling friend Emily had told him that magic didn't exist, but if Pa had actually *felt* a Smalling spell ... well, sometimes Muncle didn't know what to believe.

The cows were charging back towards the gate now – with Pa and Gritt in hot pursuit.

At the last minute, the cows changed direction.

So did Gritt.

But not Pa.

Squelch! Straight into a splat.

Pa's feet shot from under him, and he slid across the field on his bottom.

'Mooooo!' The cows hurried back to the far side of

the field. They almost sounded as if they were laughing.

'Why don't you creep up quietly behind them?' Muncle suggested.

'CREEP?' roared Pa. 'Hunters don't CREEP!'

'You may be the new Wise Man, Muncle,' said Gritt, 'but Pa's the one who knows about hunting.'

'That's right!' cried Pa, struggling to his feet, and he and Gritt charged after the herd once more.

Muncle hadn't got used to being the new Wise Man yet. He might have saved the giants by making the silly Smallings think Mount Grumble was a volcano – even though giants knew mountains couldn't blow up! – but he'd only just left school, so it felt a bit frightening to have such an important job.

Besides, he didn't really feel wise enough yet. He still had a lot of Wiseness to learn. Maybe this was a good place to start.

He wandered off and looked into the next field. The animals here were a lot smaller, not much bigger than sheep. They looked so funny with their little horns and wispy beards that Muncle couldn't help laughing at them.

'Bleeeeh!' one of the animals laughed back, leaning over the fence and taking a bite out of Muncle's

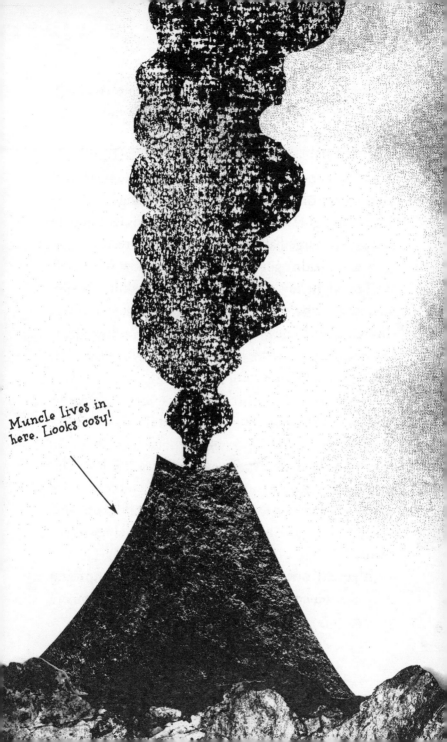

Muncle lives in here. Looks cosy!

breeches. Now it was Muncle's turn to run away. His clothes were ragged enough already – he didn't want any more holes.

He trotted across the farmyard. Birds scattered squawking from under his feet. They were bigger and fatter than pigeons, and Muncle thought about trying to hunt them, but he wasn't quick enough to catch one.

At the other side of the yard some even funnier-looking animals peered at him over the top of a wall. They had round pink faces, blunt noses and floppy ears. Muncle went over to them cautiously, but these animals didn't seem interested in biting him. They were too busy rooting about with their noses in the mud of their small pen. Some were bigger than others, but they were all plump with short legs and smooth skin, and just a few bristles here and there – a bit like giants' skin, only pink not grey. Muncle had never seen anything like them. And they smelled as lovely as Ma's perfume!

Hearing sudden footsteps behind him, Muncle spun round in alarm before he remembered that the Smallings had run away. It was only Pa. He was panting, his clothes were covered with splats, and sweat trickled down his face, which had turned from grey to purple. His net was empty.

'Didn't you get one?' said Muncle.

Pa shrugged. 'I ... ah ... changed my mind,' he said. 'Don't reckon they'd be tasty after all.'

'Why not?'

'I can just tell. Hunter's instinct. Ah, you've found the pigs.'

'These are *pigs*? You told Princess Puglug pigs looked like Smallings.'

'Well they *do* – they're smooth and pink.'

Gritt came limping across the yard. His face was even more purple than Pa's. 'Oh, we must be able to catch one of *those*, Pa,' he said, looking into the pen. 'They can't run away.'

'Catching a cow would have been just as easy, Gritt,' Pa said, sharply. 'I just decided not to. Now then, the Princess wanted a pig for a pet, didn't she?'

'She didn't want an *animal*,' said Muncle. 'She wanted a Smalling, like Emily.'

'Emily?' said Gritt, looking guilty. 'You mean the Smalling I kidnap ... er ... the Smalling Titan gave the King for his Birthday supper?'

Muncle shuddered, remembering how Gritt and Titan Bulge – Mount Grumble's worst bully – had kidnapped his Smalling friend, and how the King had nearly roasted her. It was Muncle who had helped her to escape. Nobody knew about that, though – and it had to stay that way.

'Pigs may just be animals,' said Pa, 'but don't they smell nice? Almost as nice as splats. Reminds me of your ma.'

Muncle studied the smallest pig. It *looked* nice too, with its tiny, curly tail, and little eyes that peeped out shyly from under its floppy ears. Puglug might still like it, even if it wasn't as Smallingy as she was expecting. And if she had a pig, maybe she'd forget she'd once wanted Muncle for a pet.

He scrambled over the wall and scooped up a little one, handing it out to Pa. It squealed and wriggled as Pa wrapped it up tightly in his hunting net.

'Can we take another one for supper?' said Gritt, helping Muncle back over the wall.

'No!' said Muncle. 'No, we can't eat pets. It would be like eating a dragon.'

'Then what *is* for supper? We're supposed to be hunting but we haven't caught anything yet.'

'Your ma's already making supper,' said Pa. 'Look.' He pointed to the distant top of Mount Grumble, where plumes of smoke were rising into the air. 'Everyone's got their cooking fires going. It's later than I thought. We'd better get back. Do you want to carry

Muncle or the pig, Gritt?'

'I'd rather have the pig,' said Gritt, grabbing it from Pa and setting off at top speed. He was never late for supper.

Pa swung Muncle on to his shoulders and followed Gritt up the mountain. Riding on Pa's shoulders was very uncomfortable. Pa liked jumping over boulders, and all the bouncing made Muncle feel quite sick! He clutched Pa's ears.

They left the farmland and started to climb Mount Grumble. Muncle looked up. A thick grey cloud sat on the mountain top. He felt a chill run up his spine, which was funny as it was quite a hot day.

'Pa,' he asked, 'is there always as much smoke as that?'

'People must be baking for the Victory Feast as well as cooking supper,' Pa puffed.

'You don't think—?' said Muncle, remembering what Emily had said about mountains that were really volcanoes.

Pa chuckled. 'No, I don't, Wise Man Muncle. *You're* the one who does the thinking round here.'

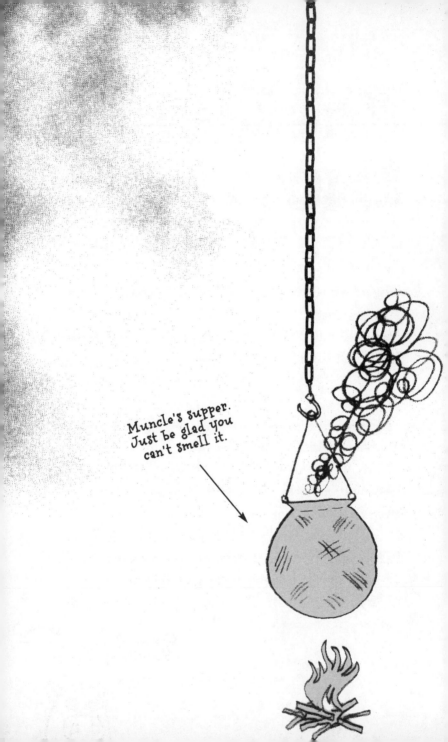

Muncle's supper.
Just be glad you
can't smell it.

Chapter two

'You've been a long time,' Ma said when they got home. She was stirring what smelt like rook-and-rabbit stew. Flubb was already asleep in her cradle. 'What's happened to your breeches, Muncle? And what the thrumbles have you got there? I'm not sure I know how to cook *that*.'

'It's not to eat,' Muncle said hurriedly. He peeled off his jerkin in the warm room. 'It's a pig for Princess Puglug, a new pet, so she won't want to play with me.' He shuddered as he remembered Puglug's rough games and, even worse, her sloppy kisses.

He quickly made a collar and lead from a length of Pa's hunting rope, and tied the pig to a hook in the wall. The pig squealed. Flubb woke up and joined in.

'What a racket!' said Ma, popping a toadstool

Say Hi to Piglitt ...

dummy into Flubb's mouth. 'I hope it's not staying long.' After a moment's thought she popped another toadstool into the pig's mouth. It gobbled it up and seemed to calm down. 'That's better. So what *have* you brought for me to cook?'

There was an uncomfortable silence. Pa and Gritt shuffled their feet.

'*Nothing*,' Muncle said, when it was obvious that Pa and Gritt weren't going to answer.

'Nothing?'

'Hunting's really difficult, Ma,' said Gritt. 'The animals just run away when you try to catch them.'

Ma looked at Pa in astonishment. 'But you've always been able to catch wild animals,' she said. 'Tame ones ought to be even easier.'

Tutting with disappointment, she ladled stew into three large bowls and one small one (for Muncle), dropping an acorn-bread roll into each bowl with a splash. They all sat down at the stone table, Muncle on his bracken-filled cushion so he could reach.

'Maybe daylight hunting isn't such a good idea after all,' he said, licking the gravy off his roll. 'The animals can see you coming. It must be easier at night, when they're asleep.'

Ma's stews are full of wormy goodness.

Pa sighed. 'That's not the trouble, Muncle. The Smallings must have put a spell on their animals before they left.'

Gritt had already gobbled up his stew. 'Is there any more?' he asked.

'You can have acorn rolls,' said Ma. 'Soak them in the water pot first, though. They're a bit stale.'

Gritt took two rolls to the huge pot where Ma stored their water supply.

'There's no room,' he said. 'The pot's full of something already.' He pulled out some soggy cloth. 'Looks like those Smalling clothes Muncle borrowed from the museum.'

'*What*?' Muncle shot off his cushion.

'I thought I ought to wash the mud off before they went back to the museum,' said Ma, 'but I don't know much about washing. Have I done it wrong?'

'*Flimflams*! Get them out, Gritt, quick!'

Startled, Gritt dumped the dripping clothes on the floor.

Muncle grabbed the breeches and fumbled frantically in the back pocket. Then he fumbled more frantically in the side pockets. Finally, in desperation, he tried the waistcoat pockets.

'It must have dropped out,' he said, his voice choked with worry. 'Can you reach to the bottom of the pot, Gritt?'

'There's nothing else in there,' said Gritt. 'Just water.'

Muncle threw himself to the floor and buried his head in his hands.

'What is it?' said Ma, kneeling down beside him. 'What are you looking for?'

'It belonged to the King!' Muncle wailed. 'I was supposed to treat it with the Utmost Respect! Biblos will never forgive me! I'll lose my job!'

'Lose your job?' growled Pa. 'Why?'

'The King will change his mind about making me Wise Man when he hears that I've lost the Book!'

'The *Book*?' gasped Ma.

'The *Book*?' cried Pa.

'The what?' said Gritt.

'The Book is the most precious thing in the museum,' explained Ma. 'It's got all the Smallings' magic spells in it.'

Gritt was excited. 'Like how to make killing sticks?'

'Well, that's what Biblos thinks,' said Muncle. 'But Emily said it was just full of recipes for Smalling food. She said there's no such thing as Smalling magic.'

Ma still looked worried, but Pa and Gritt roared with laughter. Even Flubb joined in.

'No such thing as magic?' said Pa. 'Everyone knows that magic is the only way Smallings can beat giants. But how come you had the Book in the first place?'

'Biblos kept it in the pocket of these breeches where it was found all those years ago.'

'Perhaps you needn't tell Biblos,' said Ma. She wrung the clothes out and hung them up next to the plants she was drying for medicines. Ma was much better at making medicine than washing clothes.

'I don't want to lie to him,' said Muncle. 'He's been so nice. Only Biblos could have persuaded the King to make me Wise Man.'

'It probably dropped out of your pocket when Gritt upside-downed you in the Crater,' said Pa. He glared at Gritt. 'Look at the trouble you've caused.'

'Sorry, Muncle,' said Gritt, and he actually sounded as if he meant it.

There was more bad news the next morning.

'What's the matter?' said Muncle, alarmed by the expression on Ma's face.

'The Smalling clothes,' said Ma, holding up a tiny

grey rag. 'They're not as muddy as they were, but they're not as big as they were either.'

Ma looked so upset that Muncle struggled to find the right words. 'Don't worry,' he said, trying not to look shocked. The white shirt was now about the right size for an elf.

'Will you get into trouble?' asked Gritt, who knew a thing or two about being in trouble.

Ma looked even more upset.

Muncle sat down and played with his fungus porridge. 'No more trouble than I'm in already,' he said. 'The Book's more important than the clothes.'

'Can Biblos tell you off, now you're the Wise Man and he's not?' asked Gritt. 'What are you going to tell him?'

'I don't know!' Muncle groaned. He finished his porridge in silence, trying not to think about the Book.

'What have you done to that pig, Ma?' he said then. 'It's gone very quiet.'

Flubb and the little snuffling pig were rolling happily together on the floor.

'Gave it some porridge,' said Ma. 'The Smallings must have left it without food when they ran away.'

'Sorry, Flubb,' Muncle said, trying to pick up the

pig, 'but I have to take it to Princess Puglug now.'

Flubb wailed and held on to the pig tightly. She was very strong for her age.

'I'd have brought you one too, if I'd known you'd like it so much. Perhaps we can go back and get another.'

'No! I couldn't afford to feed it!' said Ma, giving the used breakfast bowls a quick lick clean with her purple tongue before putting them away on the shelf. 'It's eaten more fungus porridge this morning than you eat in a week.'

'It even ate my seconds,' complained Gritt.

Muncle held out Flubb's bottle of fungus porridge. Flubb let go of the pig and grabbed the bottle. Muncle let go of the bottle and grabbed the pig.

'I hope the Princess will like it as much as Flubb does,' he said, anxiously. 'I just wish it looked more like a Smalling.'

'Smallings wear clothes,' said Gritt, his mouth full. He'd found a stale roll that the pig had missed.

'I've got some baby clothes that Flubb has grown out of,' said Ma.

'Then it'd look like a *giant*,' said Muncle. 'I've got a better idea.'

Clamping the pig under one arm, he grabbed the

shrunken Smalling shirt and pulled it over the pig's head. All four legs with their blunt feet disappeared inside. Now you couldn't see that the pig didn't have fingers or toes. He wrapped the sleeves round the little animal to stop it wriggling so much, and tied them together on top of its head to form a sort of hat. Now you couldn't see its floppy ears. Its snuffly snout still looked more like a dragon's nose than a Smalling's, but that couldn't be helped.

'Shouldn't you be taking that shirt back to the museum?' said Ma.

Muncle sighed. 'I can't take it back like that. I'll take the pig to the palace first. Maybe by the time I've done that I'll have thought what I'm going to tell Biblos about the clothes and the Book.'

'I'll come with you,' said Gritt, 'to make sure you're not bullied.' His eyes lit up. 'I can be the Wise Man's Bodyguard.'

'No, you can't,' said Pa. 'You've got to go to school. Anyway, no one will bully your brother if he's wearing the Wise Man's Chain. Bring it here, Muncle, and I'll make it the right size for you. It's much too long.'

Of all the precious things Biblos had entrusted to Muncle, the Wise Man's Chain, made of purest dragon gold, was the *most* precious. And the most important. If he was wearing the Chain, he could give orders to any giant in Mount Grumble.

Muncle handed the pig to Gritt and went into his bedroom. He pulled the Chain out from under his bracken mattress and sighed with relief. At least *that* was still safe. He brushed off bits of bracken and hauled it back into the kitchen. It felt as heavy as Ma's water pot and reached all the way to his ankles when he put it round his neck. He'd be glad when Pa had chopped most of it off.

Gritt gave the pig to Ma and knelt down to peer at the badge on the Chain. 'So that's what a Wonder Donkey looks like,' he said. 'At school they tell you it's the cleverest of all the animals, and the only one you must never eat, but they don't tell you what it looks like. Have you ever seen one, Pa?'

'If I had, we wouldn't be hiding underground now. A Wonder Donkey's wonders are stronger than Smalling magic. But no-one's ever seen one round here. They're as rare as the Bright Blue Badger of Back of Beyond.' Pa was trying to choose between a saw and an axe. He only had tools for hunting or cutting down trees.

Muncle could see the job was going to take him some time. 'I'll be all right without the Chain,' he said. 'All the bullies who used to be in my class will be too busy starting their new jobs today to bother with me.'

'Except for Titan Bulge,' said Ma, happily. 'He's safely in the dungeons. So he won't be getting Gritt into trouble again, either.'

'Oh, I'm finished with Titan,' said Gritt. 'I don't want to be in the Thunder Thugs any more. I want to be in *Muncle's* gang.'

'I don't have a gang,' said Muncle. 'It's not what Wise Men do.'

'And what seven-year-olds do is go to school,' said Pa. 'It's time you were off, Gritt.'

'Please let me carry the pig, Muncle,' pleaded Gritt. Full of porridge and snug in its new shirt, the pig had fallen asleep in Ma's arms and Gritt took it from her carefully, without waking it. 'I can walk with you as far as the Crater, can't I?'

Muncle was touched that Gritt wanted to help. He'd been really thoughtful since Muncle had saved him from the dungeons. He even walked slowly, so that Muncle didn't have to run to keep up.

Chapter three

It was already busy in the Crater. Dipso Drooling was setting up a barrel of Acorn Ale outside the Slurp and Slobber, while his wife Dodo arranged a counter of tempting bar snacks – pickled pigeons, toadstool toasties, caterpillar crisps and squirrels-on-sticks. On the far side of the Crater, the one-eyed waitress was dragging tables out of MuckGristle's Grubhouse and putting up parasols made out of branches. Several school-boys had stripped off their jerkins and were splashing each other under the Crater pump.

'What's going on?' Muncle asked Dipso. 'Are those boys *washing*?'

'Of course not,' laughed Dipso. 'They're just trying to cool off, though it's not easy – the water's as warm as my ale.' He took a deep breath. 'It smells nice, though, doesn't it? Just like the Farts Competition.'

'I'm thinking of splashing some of that water on myself,' said Dodo. 'It's free, and it smells as good as expensive perfume.'

'Good idea,' said Dipso with a chuckle. 'You might pull in some extra customers. We're setting up the bar here because it's so hot indoors. I've never known a summer like it.'

Boioioing! The school gong rang out.

'Jimbobs, I'm late!' Gritt threw the pig back to Muncle and ran.

The pig woke up and started to squeal.

'Ssh,' said Muncle, rocking it soothingly like the baby it wasn't as he walked towards the palace. He was too busy looking at the pig to notice a giant in a brand-new soldier's uniform step right in front of him.

'Look where you're going, you stupid minikin,' growled a familiar voice. 'You're supposed to move aside for soldiers of the King's Guard.'

Muncle looked up ...

It's one way of staying cool ...

and up ... and up ...

'Titan?' he gasped. 'How did ... how did you ... ?'

'How did I get out of the dungeons?' said Titan Bulge with a sneer. 'Pardoned by the King, of course.'

Muncle didn't believe that for a moment. It was the King who'd sent Titan to the dungeons in the first place. No, Titan's pa – who was just like Titan but bigger and nastier – must have bribed the dungeon guards.

Muncle wasn't at all happy to find that Titan was free, but Titan, who usually pounced on him with glee, didn't seem very happy either. He was shuffling from one foot to the other and looking very uncomfortable. Puzzled, Muncle looked down again. Titan was carrying his brand-new soldier's boots, not wearing them, and the reason why was clear – his feet were black and covered in blisters. Ouch.

'Did you burn your feet in the dungeons?' Muncle asked, remembering the orange Central Heating Goo he'd seen oozing up through the floor of Gritt's cell when he'd rescued him.

Titan's bushy eyebrows drew together in a scowl. 'My feet are as tough as the rest of me. They don't hurt at all. I'm still fit enough for the King's Guard. And if

Don't cross the piglitt!

you tell *anyone* I'm not, I'll tell everyone that you play with dolls,' he said, jabbing a fat finger into the little pig's belly.

The pig sank its teeth into the finger.

'Aargh! What sort of doll is *that*?'

'A ... um ... magic doll,' said Muncle. 'I found it when I went hunting on a Smalling farm.'

'*Magic? Hunting? Smalling farm?*' spluttered Titan, sucking his finger, as Muncle hurried off. '*You?*'

Muncle didn't get as far as the palace. As he passed the museum, a quavery voice called down the steps.

'Muncle! I've been looking out for you. It's time for your first Wise Man job.'

It was Biblos, leaning heavily on his stick and fanning himself with his ear-trumpet. Muncle's heart sank. He still hadn't worked out what to tell Biblos about the Book, and he certainly hadn't wanted him to see a pig wrapped in the museum's Smalling shirt. Hiding as much of the pig as he could in his jerkin, he scrambled up the steps. For some reason a King's Guardsman was on duty outside the door.

Muncle followed the old man through the dust and shadows to his desk at the back of the museum, where the reason for the King's Guardsman suddenly became clear.

'Here he is,' said Biblos, to a smaller, splendidly-dressed person who was already sitting there. 'Here's your new teacher.'

'*Him*?' screeched Princess Puglug. 'The *minikin*? He's the new *Wise Man*? He's my *teacher*?'

The Wise Man's Chain

Chapter four

'*Teacher*?' gasped Muncle. He'd only just stopped being at school himself. How could he possibly be anyone's teacher?

'Didn't I did tell you?' said Biblos. 'Being private tutor to Her Hugeness is one of the duties of the Wise Man. She is, of course, much too royal to go to school with ordinary giants.'

'No, you *didn't* tell me,' said Muncle in a panic. He thought about saying there and then that he'd lost the Book and ruined the Smalling clothes, and wasn't fit to be Wise Man after all.

Puglug's pigtails quivered with anger and her eyebrows bumped into each other as she glared at him. Then her fierce black eyes fell on the pig.

'What's *that*?' she said, pointing.

'Yes,' said Biblos, peering short-sightedly. 'What is it? Tell us, Muncle.'

Muncle thought quickly. He flashed his yellow teeth in his loveliest smile. 'It's your first lesson, Your Hugeness. This,' he announced importantly, 'is a *pig*.'

'Flittering flitflots!' exclaimed Biblos. He'd obviously never seen one before either, and didn't seem to recognise the tiny grey shirt. 'I remember someone saying that pigs were like Smallings, but I didn't realise that meant they wore clothes. Remarkable.'

Puglug's eyes opened wide and she forgot to sulk. 'A pig?' she cried. 'Like the pet Pa said he'd get me after the Smalling escaped?'

'Yes, Your Hugeness,' said Muncle. 'This *is* your new pet, if you'd like it. BUT ...' he warned as Puglug leapt towards the pig, 'it's just a baby, so you must handle it very gently.'

He lowered it slowly to the floor. The pig at once tried to run away, but could only shuffle, because all four feet were inside the shirt.

'You told me pigs were like Smallings,' said Puglug sharply. 'Why isn't it walking on two legs?'

'It's a *baby*,' Muncle said, thinking quickly again. 'It can only crawl.'

'Ah, you cute little baby piggy Smalling,' said Puglug, scooping it into her arms.

The pig looked up into Puglug's fierce black eyes.

'Oink,' it said. It looked scared.

Puglug grinned. 'Oink to you too,' she said, and squeezed the pig in a bone-crushing hug.

'*Oink*,' gasped the pig.

'Oh, you're *much* more fun than that silly Smalling,' Puglug cried. 'You're coming home with me right now. I shall call you Piglitt. I've learnt enough for today, minikin.'

Muncle and Biblos bowed low as Puglug stomped out of the museum, the King's Guardsman marching smartly behind her.

Muncle breathed a sigh of relief. That had gone better than he could possibly have hoped. Puglug was happy with the pig, and the lesson had been far shorter than any he'd ever had at school.

'Well done, Muncle,' said Biblos, beaming. 'Excellent lesson. You'll make a fine teacher and Wise Man.'

Muncle swallowed hard and tried to find the words to tell Biblos he wasn't fit to be Wise Man at all. But they just wouldn't come.

'The King hasn't told anyone that I'm Wise Man yet,' he said instead. 'He could still change his mind.'

'I don't think so. He's going to introduce you to the whole town the day after tomorrow, at the Victory Feast.'

'Really?' Muncle felt even more worried. It would be awful if the King told the whole town he was the new Wise Man and *then* changed his mind. People would never stop making fun of him.

'Indeed he is,' said Biblos. 'And there's going to be a beauty competition too – Warts 'n' All. He's very excited about that – we haven't had a Warts 'n' All since his twenty-seventh birthday. Remember to bring the Wise Man's Chain, Muncle – I expect the King will want to hang it round your neck when he introduces you, to make a little ceremony of it. Your pa's done a good job of making it fit, I hope?'

Flimflams! If Muncle had known the King would see the altered Chain close up, he'd never have let Pa do it. He thought of Pa trying to choose between an axe and a saw, and gulped. He should have taken it to the goldsmith.

He jumped up. 'I'll be right back, Biblos.'

Muncle ran home as fast as he could. He had to

No escape from the loving embrace of Princess Puglug.

rescue the Chain before Pa made a complete botch of it, or he'd be in trouble for not treating the King's property with the Utmost Respect.

And everyone knew the punishment for that.

The dungeons!

'Whatever are you doing?' cried Muncle as he burst into the kitchen.

Pa, Ma and Flubb were on their knees in front of the fire, all purple in the face.

'Oh, Muncle, come and help us,' said Ma. 'We're trying to melt your Chain.'

They started blowing on the fire again, their round cheeks almost bursting with the effort.

'I thought Pa was going to cut it.'

Pa held up the Chain. In two pieces. 'I did,' he said proudly.

Muncle stared at it in horror. 'But Pa – the ends are all mangled!'

'That's why we're trying to soften them,' said Ma, 'so we can bend them back.'

'Pa, you've got to get it mended!'

Pa scratched his head and sighed. 'I'll have to take it to Bruzer Biffit,' he said.

'Your friend at the Iron Works?'

'That's him. He can melt anything. He doesn't even need a fire any more. He just uses the Goo that's coming up through the floor.'

'Pa, Bruzer goes to the Slurp and Slobber every night. And he can talk the hind leg off a donkey. If he sees we've damaged the Chain everyone will hear about it, and then we'll all be thrown in the dungeons.'

Pa and Ma went pale.

Muncle took the Chain and stuffed it into one of Pa's hunting sacks. 'I've got a friend who can melt gold too,' he said, 'and *he* won't tell anyone – because he can't talk.'

Muncle slipped quietly out of Mount Grumble by the broken gate he always used, and dragged the heavy sack of gold through the forest. He didn't blow his silver dragon flute – a present from Biblos – until he reached his den, an old hut in a clearing. It was the only place in the forest where there was enough room for a dragon to land.

His old friend Snarg could produce anything from a friendly warm lick to a white-hot, rock-melting flame. He'd have no trouble softening gold.

Snarg came almost immediately. He circled above the tree tops, peering down as if to make sure it was his friend Muncle calling him, and not Mr Thwackum, the Dragon Science teacher, who might try to capture him and clip his wings again. Then he swooped to the ground.

'*Aaaargh*!' An ear-splitting scream came from inside the hut.

Startled, Muncle ran to look inside.

A small girl with yellow hair huddled trembling in a corner, her hands clasped to her face and her blue eyes wide with fear.

'Emily!' gasped Muncle. 'What the thrumbles are you doing here?'

Chapter five

Emily stumbled across the hut and clutched Muncle's hand.

'I'm so glad it's you,' she said in a shaky voice. 'I saw this huge shadow, and I thought it must be one of the proper-sized giants, although it looked more like a ... more like a ... AAAARGH!'

Snarg had stuck his head through the door. He blocked out almost all the light, except for a few rays that found their way past the cobwebs in the tiny window.

'It's all right,' said Muncle. 'It's just Snarg. He's with me.' He put his dragon flute to his lips and blew the signal for 'Lie Down'.

Snarg dropped to the floor. He gazed at Emily with interest and breathed out a flicker of flame.

'I was right,' she gasped, hiding hurriedly behind Muncle. 'It is a dragon.'

'You remember when I told you about the King's stables,' said Muncle, 'and you were surprised that we kept horses in Mount Grumble? Well, we don't. We keep dragons.'

'Can you make it go away? It's making me feel trapped, like when I was a prisoner in here.'

Muncle felt a pang of guilt. What would Emily think if she knew it was his brother who had kidnapped her, to impress Titan Bulge? At least he could make her feel better now.

'Stand up!' he blew. 'Turn Left! Plod! Stop! Lie Down!'

Snarg settled down on the far side of the clearing.

Emily tiptoed to the door and peeped out. 'Giants *and* dragons,' she whispered. 'Are there fairies and goblins round here too?'

'I'm afraid not,' said Muncle. 'They all disappeared donkey's years ago. But, Emily, what are *you* doing here? We thought all the Smallings had run away, because of the ... er ...

fire.' He felt guilty again. Should he tell her that it had been his idea to start the fire?

'It was scary, but the fire brigade stopped it reaching any houses.'

Muncle was astonished. Mount Grumble Fire Brigade had the most up-to-date fire-beating brooms, but even they would have found it hard to beat out flames as tall as oak trees. 'They must use powerful magic,' he said.

'They don't use magic,' Emily chuckled. 'They use *water*.'

'Oh.' Muncle would never have thought of doing that, but it was true that Ma's cooking fire did go out if she spilled water on it. 'So no-one ran away?' he said.

'Only overnight, until the firemen said it was safe to come back.'

'How did they know it was safe? Weren't they afraid Mount Grumble was blowing up?'

Emily laughed. 'Nobody thought that. A volcano blowing up is nothing like a forest fire.'

So he'd failed.

The Smallings hadn't believed his brilliant volcano plan. They hadn't thought the mountain was exploding.

Worst of all, they were back.

Which meant it *wasn't* safe to leave Mount Grumble in daylight.

'It was nice of you to come and warn me,' he said.

'But that isn't why I came,' said Emily. 'I didn't know you thought we'd gone away. I came to bring you this.' She pulled something out of her bag.

When Muncle saw what was in her hand, he gasped and ran to her in delight.

'The *Book*! Where did you find it?'

'Just where the town stops and the forest begins. You must have dropped it on your way home after you'd rescued me. I was going to leave it in your den for you.'

'Oh, Emily, thank you!' He hugged her.

'OUCH!'

'*Sorry*. I forgot I'm strong enough to hurt you. I'm just so pleased to get the Book back.'

Now Biblos need never know that the Book had been missing. After a quick look to make sure it wasn't damaged, Muncle pushed it deep into his pocket for safe-keeping and found something else in there. He pulled it out.

'Would you like this,' he said, 'as a thank-you present

for finding the Book?'

'What is it?'

'My old dragon flute. But don't blow it, or you may get a surprise visit from Snarg!'

'Thanks, Muncle. I'll just look at it.' Carefully, Emily put the plain pottery flute in her pink, sparkly bag.

Muncle remembered then why he'd come to the clearing in the first place. He pulled the Wise Man's Chain from his sack and took it over to the dragon.

'What are you doing?' Emily hung back as Muncle held one end of the Chain under Snarg's nose.

'Mending this. Lick, Snarg.'

Snarg looked at him blankly.

'Like this,' said Muncle, and he licked the Chain.

Snarg reached out his long orange tongue and licked Muncle's face.

Emily giggled. 'Why don't you use your whistle thingy?'

'I can't.' Muncle rubbed steaming dragon spit from his face with a handful of grass. 'There isn't a signal for "Lick". I'll have to ask him to breathe fire. Stand back, Emily.'

Muncle set the mangled ends of the Chain on some dry leaves. Then he stepped out of the way and blew

'Burn'.

A flash of white lightning shot from Snarg's nostrils with a hiss. The leaves crumpled to ash. Muncle darted forward and snatched up the Chain. Several links plopped to the ground in a blob of gold.

Flimmering flimflams! But it wasn't Snarg's fault. There was no signal to tell him to 'Burn Red-Hot' rather than 'Burn White-Hot'. And at least the lost links were the mangled ones. The Chain did now look as if it had been cut in two by an expert.

Muncle patted Snarg on the nose and carried the Chain to the hut. He found some bits of string among the treasures he kept there, and used them to tie the ends of the shorter bit of Chain. Then he hung it round his shoulders with the string underneath his jerkin and the Wonder Donkey badge in full view on his chest.

'There,' he said. 'How does that look? Can you tell it's broken?'

'No,' said Emily. 'It looks fine. But what is it?'

'It's the Wise Man's Chain,' Muncle said, explaining that he'd been given a grand new job because of his good ideas.

'Oh!' Emily looked rather surprised. 'I mean, good for you. But why is there a picture of a horse on it?'

'It's not a horse,' said Muncle. 'It's a Wonder Donkey, the cleverest creature on earth.'

'It *is*?' Emily laughed.

'Thank you so much for the Book and for telling me the Smallings have come back,' Muncle said. 'Now I really must go home quickly to warn everyone. At least the message will get round quickly, with so many people in the Crater together.'

'Are you having another party?'

'No, it's just cooler outside.'

Emily frowned. 'But it should be cooler *inside*. You live underground. I went into some caves on holiday last year and felt really cold, even though it was a hot day.'

'It *used* to feel really cold,' said Muncle. 'I always had to sit right by the fire to get warm. But now Ma lets the fire go out unless she's cooking, and I still don't feel cold. It's strange, because although there aren't so many fires these days the town always seems to be full of smoke.'

Emily frowned. 'The mountain is getting warmer and smokier?'

Muncle looked deep into her blue eyes. They looked very serious. 'Yes ...' he said, hesitantly. 'Why are you looking so worried, Emily?'

Emily shook her head. 'I can't explain well enough, Muncle. I need to find out more first. But can you meet me here at the same time tomorrow? It could be important.'

Is it a bit dusty in here?

Chapter six

Muncle watched Emily disappear among the trees as she followed the stream back to the Smalling town. He'd never expected to see her again and he'd forgotten how nice she was.

He hadn't liked that worried look in her eyes, though. He felt sure she was thinking about volcanoes again. Were they just a Smalling myth, or could they possibly be real? It was a terrifying thought. He closed his eyes, rubbed the wart on his right thumb and made a wish – that whatever she found out would be good news.

He checked the position of the sun so that he could be sure of coming back at the same time next day. Then he climbed on to Snarg's back, finding footholds on his scales with his small bare toes, and flew back to Mount

Grumble. It was the quickest way home – and he had urgent news to deliver.

Everyone would be so disappointed that the Smallings were back. And what would happen to the Victory Feast? But the most important thing was to warn everyone not to leave Mount Grumble in daylight.

He circled over the Crater several times, but couldn't persuade Snarg to land. He was probably remembering Mr Thwackum's dragon-shears. Down below them, Muncle could see a large crowd of women pushing and shoving round one of the market stalls. What was going on?

He kept blowing a new signal he'd made up to mean 'Land', and followed it with 'Sit' and 'Lie Down' to help Snarg understand what it meant. At last Snarg *did* land, but high up on the Crater rim, not down among all the giants.

'There's nothing to be afraid of,' Muncle told him. 'Now I'm Wise Man I'm not going to let anyone lock you in a stable or clip your wings.'

But Snarg wouldn't go any nearer. Muncle had to slide off his back and scramble down the steep track that led into the Crater, dragging the heavy sack of spare gold behind him.

But although he had important news for the Town Crier to announce, and although he was now wearing the Wise Man's Chain, he still didn't feel confident about giving orders until they'd been agreed by Biblos. He buttoned his jerkin to hide his Chain and stop people asking awkward questions.

As he hurried to the museum, the Troggs' neighbour, Mrs Bashpot, fought her way out of the crowd. She was looking very pleased with herself.

'What's going on?' Muncle asked her.

'Fans,' she said, shaking a bundle of jackdaw feathers at him. For a moment a cool breeze blew across his face. 'Queen Fattipat was waving one at the King's Birthday and now everyone wants one. It's so *hot* ...'

It would take a lot of feathers to blow a cool breeze over Mount Grumble at the moment, Muncle thought, as he trudged up the museum steps.

'Muncle!' cried Biblos with his mouth full. He was tucking into a dish of stuffed stoats, a takeaway from

MuckGristle's. 'You left in a terrible hurry – is something wrong?'

'Yes,' said Muncle, seizing the chance not to explain why he'd really left in a hurry. 'Very wrong. The Smallings are back.'

'*What*? How do you know?'

Muncle could hardly admit that he'd just been talking to one. 'I've just seen them in the forest,' he said. 'And lots of carts are moving on their roads again.'

'So we haven't got a victory to celebrate after all,' said Biblos, sadly.

Muncle had been thinking about this on his way home. 'Well, we haven't frightened the Smallings away for ever,' he said, 'but we did stop them finding our town gates. We stopped them finding us. That's something to celebrate.'

Biblos cheered up again. 'You're right, Muncle,' he said. 'We can have a Victory Feast after all. Now have some dinner quickly and then you must go and buy me a fan. It's very warm in the museum nowadays.' He picked up the end of his beard and used it to wipe the sweat from his forehead and the gravy from the tip of his nose.

It *was* warm. Muncle put his heavy sack down in a

corner and unfastened his jerkin. 'I must tell the Town Crier to announce a daylight hunting ban before I do anything else,' he said, taking a quick bite of stoat.

'Oh, Muncle, how do you manage to think about so many things at once?' Biblos scratched his head with a stoat bone. 'You really are brilliant. Off you go!'

Muncle took a second stoat, hurried out of the museum – and found people weren't enjoying their outdoor dinner much after all. They were coughing, sneezing and waving their hands about, and Muncle could only see them dimly.

It was as if a grey curtain had been drawn across the Crater while he'd been in the museum. He hunched his shoulders and pulled his jerkin up around his ears, expecting the air to be cold and damp with fog. But it wasn't. It was warm and dry and had the same sort of smell that he'd noticed in the dungeons.

'What's happening?' he asked the woman at the first market stall he came to.

'I saw someone taking an enormous ox into MuckGristle's,' the woman said, trying to waft the thick grey air away with her hands. 'I think he must have burnt it.'

'Nonsense,' said another stall-holder, busily licking

clean her stock of bluebottle biscuits and cockroach cookies. 'This isn't smoke. The King's Guard were practising their marching for the Victory Feast and suddenly there was dust everywhere.'

Muncle ran to the Barracks of the King's Guard. A crowd of people had gathered in front of it, and they were all shouting at one man. It took a moment for Muncle to recognise the Captain, who normally wore a splendid purple tunic. Like everyone else, he was covered from head to toe in grey dust.

'It wasn't my fault, I tell you,' protested the Captain. '*We* didn't kick this dust up. It just whooshed out through the windows of our Barracks.'

'Balderdash!' The Town Crier seized the Captain and shook him till the dust fell off. 'Why would dust suddenly whoosh out of windows when it's never done so before?'

The Town Crier was one of the scariest giants in Mount Grumble, because the man with the loudest voice was always given the job, and the loudest voice always belonged to the biggest giant with the biggest belly.

'How should I know?' said the unhappy Captain. 'That's a question for the Wise Man. Let's go and ask him.'

He took a step backwards and tripped over Muncle.

'Looks like the Wise Man is here already,' chuckled the Town Crier. He bent down as far as his belly would allow, picked Muncle up and waved him about, Chain clanking, for the crowd to see. Everyone laughed. 'You made a good Smalling in the King's Birthday play, minikin,' he boomed, in a voice that shook the Crater walls, 'but you make a perfectly ridiculous Wise Man, so take off that pretend Chain and get back to school.'

'It's not pretend,' Muncle protested. 'I've brought an order from Biblos. You're to announce that daylight hunting is banned.'

The Town Crier laughed so much that he dropped Muncle. 'Do you hear that, everyone? We have to take our orders from the Town Wibblewit!'

'It's an order from *Biblos*!' Muncle said again, but his voice was croaky with dust and they didn't hear him above the laughter. He didn't mind being called a minikin, but he hated being called a wibblewit. His wits were a lot less wibbly than most giants'. He cleared his throat. 'All right!' he shouted, fighting his way through the ankles of the crowd. 'Don't listen to me! But when hunters are hurt by Smalling killing sticks

it'll be your fault.'

'Killing sticks?' squeaked the Captain. 'Did you say killing sticks?'

'Yes,' said Muncle. 'The Smallings are back.'

'What?' said the Captain faintly.

'Smallings are back?' cried one of his men, waving his battle-axe. 'Hooray! It wasn't fair that the Dragon Division got all the fighting in the Great Smalling Battle. And they messed it up. Let the Heavy Brigade get at 'em!'

'Hooray!' echoed the rest of the soldiers. 'An even Greater Smalling Battle!'

'THERE. WILL. BE. NO. FIGHTING!' Muncle shouted, but no-one was listening.

'Fighting?' The Captain had gone very pale.

'Don't tell me you're taking this minikin seriously, Captain,' barked the Town Crier. 'Can't you see he's play-acting again?'

'I'm not sure,' said the Captain, who never seemed very sure about anything. 'Biblos did use him to send me orders in the Great Smalling Battle. He could be doing it again. It's better to be safe than sorry.'

He picked Muncle up by the scruff of the neck and carried him across the Crater and up the museum steps.

Biblos was lighting candles as the Captain pushed Muncle through the door.

'Ah, Muncle,' he said. 'It's turned into a terribly dull day. I hate it when the Crater's full of cloud.'

'Nod gloud,' Muncle croaked.

'What?' Biblos adjusted his ear trumpet.

'*Yaargh.*' Muncle cleared his throat again. 'Sorry. I said it's not cloud. It's dust.' He coughed and rubbed his eyes.

The Captain edged into the museum. 'You were expecting this minik ... er ... this young giant, Your Wiseness?' he asked nervously.

'Well of course I was,' said Biblos. 'He works here.'

'So you really meant the Town Crier to announce a daylight hunting ban?'

'Flittering flitflots, hasn't he done it yet? Go and give him the order again. No time to lose. The Smallings are back!'

'Buggling buglugs!' muttered the Captain faintly, and he ran down the museum steps on shaky legs just as the one-eyed waitress from MuckGristle's arrived with a pot of nettle tea for Biblos.

'That was quick,' said Biblos. 'I've only just ordered it.'

'Water's not as cold as it used to be, Your Wiseness,' she said, 'so it boils quicker.' She shut the door as she left to stop more dust blowing in.

'How useful,' said Biblos. 'Hot water straight from the pump. Life is getting easier in Mount Grumble.' He poured a cup of tea for Muncle. 'Drink this,' he said. 'It'll clear the dust from your throat. Then you must tell me where you think all this dust has suddenly come from.'

chapter seven

That night, Muncle was woken by a loud rattling noise. It wasn't like the regular soothing sound of snoring Troggs, and it kept stopping and starting. It must be Pa, hammering something. But why, when he should be out night-time hunting? Muncle got up and went to ask him to stop.

It was dark in the main room. No-one was there. The hammering was coming from somewhere under the floor. Muncle went back to bed and tore bits of bracken out of his mattress to stuff in his ears.

The noise was even worse at breakfast the next morning.

CLONK. CLONK. RATTATATTAT. CLONK.

'They're at it again!' cried Ma. 'Those Bashpots are always putting up new shelves.'

Banging
brain ache.

'It's been going on all night.' Muncle rubbed his forehead, which ached from lack of sleep. 'It's even louder in my room.'

'I'll go down and speak to them after breakfast. They shouldn't be making a row like that at night.'

Muncle finished his porridge, then fetched his Chain from under his mattress and put it on.

'Are you off already?' said Ma.

'I mustn't be late for work,' Muncle lied. What he was really afraid of was being late for Emily. He didn't want to miss her. She'd looked so worried yesterday when he mentioned that Mount Grumble was getting warmer and smokier. He needed to know what she'd found out. Was she going to tell him that *he* ought to be worried too?

Gritt was only halfway through his second helping of porridge and had three rolls lined up beside his bowl for his next course. 'But I haven't finished my breakfast,' he said.

'Don't worry,' said Muncle. 'I'm sure I'll be all right without a bodyguard for one day.'

When Muncle came out of the street-tunnel he discovered that it had rained in the night and washed all the dust out of the air. He could see across the Crater clearly this morning.

Unfortunately this meant he could also *be seen*.

He'd only gone a few steps when a King's Guardsman in a smart new uniform pounced on him, grabbing Muncle by his jerkin and banging him against the rocky wall.

Thumper Plodd, Titan's best friend.

'Harder, Thumper,' said a voice, and Titan hobbled out of the shadows. 'Give him a good bashing for telling the Captain about my burnt feet.'

'I haven't told the Captain anything,' Muncle protested.

'You must have. I got the highest ever mark in Martial Arts in my Gigantia exam. Why else would he throw me out of the King's Guard?'

'Because you're limping?' Muncle suggested.

'I. AM. NOT. LIMPING!' shouted Titan. He snatched Muncle out of Thumper's hands and bounced him on the ground. 'Now I'm going to tell everyone about your doll, minikin.'

'It wasn't *my* doll,' said Muncle. 'It was a present for Princess Puglug.'

Thumper sniggered. 'Oooh, a present for Her

Titan Bulge
(he's actually
even less nice
than he looks)

Hugeness.'

Titan picked Muncle up by the ears. 'Why are you giving presents to the Princess, minikin? Is she your girlfriend?'

'PUT HIM DOWN!'

It was Gritt, and he was full of fungus porridge.

Titan spun round on his blistered foot, yelped with pain and fell to the ground. Muncle sailed through the air.

Gritt caught him and put him down – gently for once. Then he turned to Titan, bending over him with clenched fists. The biggest seven-year-old in Mount Grumble was surprisingly scary when he wanted to be.

'IF YOU EVER TOUCH MY BROTHER AGAIN, TITAN BULGE, YOU'LL END UP BACK IN THE DUNGEONS. YOU CAN'T TREAT HIM LIKE THAT NOW HE'S THE WISE MAN!'

Now Thumper didn't just snigger. He roared with laughter.

'Don't you dare laugh at me!' Titan yelled, as he struggled to get up.

'I wasn't,' said Thumper. 'I was laughing at the idea of Muncle Trogg being Wise Man.'

For a moment Muncle, who had sat down to

recover, thought that the funny feeling in his bottom was Thumper's laughter making the ground buzz. But then Thumper stopped laughing and the ground went on buzzing.

'What's that?' said Titan.

'What?' said Thumper.

'Can't you feel it? The ground is sort of ...'

'Must be your funny feet.'

'There is nothing wrong with my FEET!' Titan wrestled Thumper over and pinned his ear to the ground. The pain in his feet didn't stop him being strong. 'Now are you getting it?'

'Yes, all right, the ground's buzzing,' Thumper squeaked. He looked at Titan in alarm. 'It must be magic!' he said. 'That Smalling girl you gave the King must have put a spell on the Crater while she was here.'

'Are you saying the Smallings have magicked a nest of killer wasps under the Crater and it's MY FAULT?'

'No, Titan, of course not. I didn't mean ...'

Gritt and Muncle made a run for it, leaving Titan and Thumper arguing.

Gritt looked worried. 'Muncle, do you think that girl really has put a spell on the Crater?'

'I'm not sure.' Muncle still didn't know what to

think about magic. Could the buzzing be a spell? Or something else, but just as dangerous?

They glanced back. Titan and Thumper seemed to be friends again.

'I'd better come all the way to the museum with you,' said Gritt.

'But you'll be late for school.'

'It doesn't matter. They won't dare tell me off when they know I'm the Wise Man's brother. When is everyone going to know, Muncle?'

'Tomorrow, I think, at the Victory Feast.'

Muncle wished he could look forward to the Feast, but it was hard not to worry. What would the King make of a Wise Man's Chain held together by string? Would he really tell everyone that Muncle was his new Wise Man? And even if he did, would people take orders from a ten-year-old the size of a baby? His attempt to give an order to the Town Crier hadn't exactly been a good start.

'I can't wait to see my friends' faces when they find out,' said Gritt.

'You mean you haven't told them already?' Muncle was surprised. Gritt could spread news round Mount Grumble faster than the Town Crier.

Gritt looked uncomfortable. 'I stopped telling them after they laughed at me,' he admitted. 'It's hard being the Wise Man's brother.'

Muncle sighed. 'Not half as hard as being the Wise Man.'

Chapter eight

It was cool in the forest.

In the clearing Emily was sitting on a fallen tree trunk next to the stream, her pink sparkly bag beside her. On her lap was something amazing.

'Another book,' gasped Muncle, sitting down beside her. 'A huge book. There must be a lot of recipes in that!' Or was it more magic?

'Books aren't always about recipes, Muncle,' Emily smiled.

Muncle stared at the picture on the front, all black and red and yellow. He'd never seen anything so colourful. 'Nice bonfire,' he said.

'It's not a bonfire. You can't tell how big it is from the photo. That black shape that's on fire isn't a pile of wood – it's a volcano.'

Volcano
brain ache.

Deep inside Muncle's belly, something wriggled itself into a knot. 'A volcano?' he said. 'A volcano *blowing up*?'

'Yes.'

The whole mountain was being swallowed by fire. He stared at the picture.

'I was so worried about what you said yesterday,' Emily said, 'that I went to the library and got a book I could bring to show you. There's a chapter in it about warning signs.'

Muncle still couldn't take his eyes off the picture. 'Warnings that a mountain is really a volcano?'

'Warnings that a volcano might be about to blow up.' Emily opened the book. There were rows of squiggles all over the page. 'Warning Signs,' she said, pointing to some bigger squiggles at the top.

Muncle stared, wishing he knew how to make sense of them.

'Heat and smoke are two signs,' Emily read. 'Tell me if you've noticed any of these others. Dust clouds, hammering noises ...'

Muncle fell backwards off the tree trunk.

'Muncle! Are you all right?'

He got back on to the tree trunk feeling sick and

It's a photo of a volcano.

wobbly. 'Not really,' he said shakily. 'There was dust all over the Crater yesterday, and hammering in the night ... Emily, Mount Grumble really is a volcano, isn't it?'

'That's what I keep trying to tell you! Muncle, volcanoes can lie quiet for hundreds of years. But then they suddenly come back to life. And it looks as if Mount Grumble is coming back to life *now*.'

Muncle buried his head in his hands but the picture of the burning mountain wouldn't go away. 'I'm the Wise Man,' he said, desperately. 'It's up to me to keep everyone safe. Emily, how long have I got? How long before Mount Grumble blows up?'

Emily frowned as she turned the pages of the book. 'I don't know. It doesn't say.'

'It *must* say. Is it years or months – or days?'

'Muncle, I don't *know*. I think it's quite hard to tell.'

Muncle chewed the wart on his right thumb. 'We've got to get out, haven't we?' he said. 'Before it's too late. We're going to have to leave Mount Grumble.'

But Mount Grumble was home. He'd never known anywhere else. He didn't even know what anywhere else looked like. He bit the wart clean off his thumb and swallowed it.

Emily shut the book and looked at him. Tears shone

in her blue eyes, and Muncle realised that if Mount Grumble blew up she'd lose her home at the foot of the mountain too.

'I think you *will* have to leave,' she agreed. 'We all will. But Muncle, where can you *go*?'

'There is one place,' he said slowly. 'Back of Beyond. There are lots of stories about it. It's a land of lakes and forests full of food. Life there is easy because there are Dwelfs to do all the work, and there are no Smallings to make it dangerous. The only magic there belongs to a herd of Wonder Donkeys and they use it to help us. It's where all giants came from, long, long ago before we spread out to rule the whole world. It's where dragons come from too.'

Emily looked doubtful. 'It's a lovely story,' she said, 'but are you sure it's true? To us, "back of beyond" just means somewhere a long way from anywhere else.'

'That's exactly what it *is*. A long way away from Smallings. We'd be able to live our old way of life there, out of doors.'

'Do you know how to get there?'

'Oh, yes. You just keep going north until you can't go any further, and that's Back of Beyond.'

'Riiiight,' Emily said slowly. 'But aren't you afraid of

being hunted down by us – by Smallings – on the way?'

This was when Muncle thought of his wildest idea ever.

'We'd have to fly,' he said.

'*Fly*? How?'

'By dragon, of course. We've got enough, if each full-grown dragon carries two or three giants.'

Emily shook her head. 'I can't believe we've never seen all these dragons flying round Mount Grumble.'

Muncle drew in a deep breath and let it out again slowly. This was where his plan ran into trouble.

'That's the problem,' he said. 'They can't fly. They've all had their wings clipped.'

'Clipped? What do you mean?'

'You cut the skin between the wing-bones,' he said, 'so the wings don't work properly.'

'Ouch,' said Emily. 'Poor dragons. Were Snarg's wings ever clipped?'

Muncle shook his head. 'Gritt was supposed to clip them at school but he forgot. That's how Snarg escaped. He's living free now, like a wild dragon.'

They sat in silence for a while.

'Emily, can we really not work out how soon we need to leave?' Muncle asked. 'Are there warning signs that only happen when a mountain is about to blow up?'

Emily opened the book again. 'Yes,' she said. 'There are harm ... harm-on-ic tremors.'

'What are they?'

'I don't know. Wait while I read what it says ... Oh, sometimes you can feel the ground sort of buzzing when there's lava flowing under you.'

Muncle buried his head in his hands again and groaned.

'You've noticed that too, haven't you?' Emily said, quietly.

Muncle nodded. He hadn't imagined it. And Titan and Thumper had felt it as well. 'What's lava?' he asked.

'Melted rock. It's very thick, so it doesn't flow like water from a tap. It sort of *creeps*. Usually it's deep underground but when a volcano erupts – that's the proper word for when it blows up – the lava comes to the surface and bursts out. I've seen it on television.'

Lava. Tap. Television. There were so many new words that Muncle was finding it hard to understand what she was saying. 'Is there a drawing of lava in the book?'

'They're not drawings, Muncle.' Emily turned the pages quickly. 'They're photographs. They show exactly what a real volcano looks like. Oh, here's a good one of lava!'

Muncle looked at the picture. He felt faint. 'You didn't tell me lava was orange,' he whispered. 'Why isn't it stone-coloured, if it's melted stone?'

'It's orange because it's so hot. Muncle, what's the matter?'

He swallowed several times but couldn't move the sudden lump in his throat.

The lava in the picture looked exactly like Goo.

Chapter nine

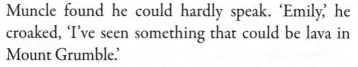

Muncle found he could hardly speak. 'Emily,' he croaked, 'I've seen something that could be lava in Mount Grumble.'

Emily drew her breath in sharply. 'Lava in your Crater? Oh, Muncle—'

'No, no, it's not in the Crater. It's deeper, down a lot of steps. In the dungeons. And Pa says it's in the Iron Works too. I'll go and fetch some. Then you can tell me if you think it's lava or not.'

'I've only seen it on television, Muncle—'

'Please, Emily. You know much more about it than I do.'

'All right, I'll have a look at it. Meet me here again tomorrow.'

'Can you really come three days in a row? Don't you

ever have to go to school?'

'Not for the next six weeks. It's the summer holidays.'

Six *weeks*! The school holiday in Mount Grumble was usually only one day – the King's Birthday – though this year there would be the extra Victory Feast too.

Emily put the book back in her pink bag. 'Be very careful getting the lava, Muncle,' she said. 'It'll be boiling hot and dangerous. And try not to worry. We've got different alerts to tell us how dangerous Mount Grumble is and at the moment it's only a Yellow Alert.'

'What other alerts are there?'

'Amber,' said Emily. 'Then red.' She paused. 'That's the last one.'

Muncle hurried back to the museum, his head throbbing with the worries that were swirling round inside. He found Biblos taking the lid off a dish of hare-and-heron hash.

'Tuck in,' said the old man.

'I'm not hungry, thanks. Biblos, what do you know about Goo?'

'Oh, it's great stuff. I hear they're using it at the Iron

Works now instead of fires, which is really useful, with wood harder to find since we burnt down half the forest.'

'You don't think it could be ...' Muncle had been going to say 'melted rock', but now he was back in Mount Grumble, with life going on as normal, it suddenly seemed such a silly idea that he wasn't sure he believed it himself, '... dangerous?' he finished, lamely.

'Well, obviously you wouldn't let a baby crawl into it,' said Biblos, 'but it's no more dangerous than a fire. Are you feeling all right, Muncle? You're looking very pale.'

'I've got a bit of a headhurt.'

'Then take the rest of the day off. You need to get your head better in case the King has some Thinking he needs you to do. But at the moment all he's interested in is the Victory Feast, and the Steward of the King's Birthday is making the arrangements for that. Are any of your family going in for Warts 'n' All?'

'Ma's having a go at Wartiest Woman. She's got more warts than anyone else I know. And Pa's trying for Most Massive Muscles. He's been out in the forest, strengthening his arms by pulling up oak trees. They're putting Flubb in for Bumpiest Baby-Bum because of all her botty-boils and rolls of fat. And Gritt's got a good chance in the Strapping Super-Sevens. He's the tallest in his class and already strong enough to use the heaviest hammer in the school metalwork room.'

'And I'm going to win Prettiest Princess!' The door flew open and Puglug burst in. Her hair stuck up in a tuft through the middle of her crown and she was carrying a bundle wrapped up in a blanket. 'You've got to keep Piglitt for me, Biblos,' she said, dumping the bundle on the floor, 'or Nursie will roast her on my bedroom fire and make me eat her for supper.'

'Why would she do that?' asked Muncle, as the bundle started to snuffle its way round the floor. Its blanket fell off to reveal a sheepskin nappy and a fancy woollen dress suitable for a royal pig.

'Yesterday Nursie spanked her for doing plops in her cradle,' said Puglug, 'and Piglitt bit her.'

Muncle grinned. He'd met Nursie, and couldn't blame Piglitt for biting her. 'But Draggly used to pee in his bed,' he said, remembering the night he'd spent with the Princess's baby dragon, 'and she let *him* stay.'

'She was glad when I got tired of him, though. Guard!' Puglug yelled. 'You can bring him in.'

A Guardsman peered round the door, then led a

very sickly baby dragon into the museum on a lead. His rainbow colours had faded, his head drooped and he could barely walk.

Draggly had been pale when Muncle saw him last. But at least he'd been able to walk well enough to take himself through the dragon flap and down the passage to the Royal Stables when he needed a pee. 'What happened to his feet?' he asked.

'Goo,' said Puglug. 'It's been coming up through the stable floor for a while now, and we've been feeding it to our Rainbow Royals instead of sunshine. But silly Draggly went and trod in it. We need to keep him somewhere where there isn't any Goo.'

Biblos shook his head. 'I'm very sorry, Your Hugeness, but they can't stay here. I'm much too old to be looking after animals.'

'I'll take them,' said Muncle. Flubb would be very happy to get Piglitt back, and Ma might just have some medicine that would heal Draggly's feet and bring the colour back to his scales.

'Remember, Wise Minikin, Piglitt's still mine,' said Puglug quickly. 'You must bring her to me every day so I can play with her.'

'Piglitt *is* still yours,' Muncle agreed, remembering

how much the little pig could eat, 'which means you'll have to pay for her food.'

'Guard, purse!' Puglug held out her hand.

The Guardsman pulled a squirrel-skin purse from his pocket and handed it over. Puglug took out a nugget – she didn't seem to have anything smaller. Muncle couldn't imagine being so rich that your pocket money came in nuggets – a hundred times more than the nugglin most children got at her age. Muncle had never got any.

'Thanks,' he said, pushing it deep into his pocket. 'That'll keep her in porridge for a nice long time.'

'How about a lesson while you're here, Your Hugeness?' said Biblos.

'Not today. I'm much too busy getting ready for the Prettiest Princess competition. I still have to try on my new ferret-fur dress and decide which crown to wear. Ma says I'm too young to wear red clay make-up, so I'll have to sneak into her room and steal some.'

Muncle walked home with Piglitt under one arm and Draggly's lead in the other hand.

An excited Flubb fell on the animals, not sure which to cuddle first.

Ma was horrified. 'Muncle, you know I can't afford to feed that pig.'

Muncle slapped the nugget down on the table. 'For porridge,' he said, 'and maybe some medicine for the dragon.'

Ma's eyes opened wide and she slid the nugget into her apron pocket. 'What's the matter with him?'

'Draggly used to be Princess Puglug's pet,' Muncle said. 'I think they gave him water to keep him quiet, and no sunshine. And his feet are burnt, but that was an accident.'

Ma knelt down and gently stroked Draggly's sensitive ears. 'Poor creature,' she said. 'If that's all it is, we'll soon have you well again.'

'You know about dragon illnesses?' Muncle was surprised. The Troggs had never had enough money to own a guard dragon.

'When I was a girl there was an old woman they called the Dragon Doctor. She sometimes came into Dragon Science classes – they were my favourite lessons. I can still remember all the illnesses she told us about, and all the cures. Except for dragonpox. Even she didn't know a cure for that.'

Draggly rolled on to his back and gazed up at her.

'At least it isn't dragonpox,' Ma said. 'His eyes would be blue if it was.'

Muncle needed curing too. His headhurt was no better. Ma gave him a dose of Willow Juice and he slept for a while. When he woke up the headhurt had gone, but not the worry. He went into the kitchen, where Draggly and Piglitt were curled up together comfortably.

'Ma, have you got a small clay bowl, with handles?'

Most of Ma's dishes were made of iron or wood and would be no good for carrying something as hot as Goo.

'I've hardly any clay at all. Why?'

'Er ... some of the things I do as Wise Man are sort of secret. I can't explain why at the moment.'

'Oh, Muncle, I can't get over you having such an important job!' Ma rummaged in the back of her cupboard. 'There's this old baby feeding cup, but it's broken – Gritt bit the spout off it when he was two weeks old.'

It was covered with cobwebs and full of dead flies. Muncle was hungry after missing his dinner and happily munched them up.

'That's perfect, thanks. I don't need the spout. I'm

going out again now, Ma, but I'll be back before supper.'

Muncle squeezed the pot into his old school bag and hurried to the Iron Works, scrambling down the steep steps.

He was greeted by the sound of hammering as he jumped down the last step into a wide, high room full of noise and smoke and heat. Bubbling sticky orange stuff oozed from cracks in the floor – the same bubbling sticky orange stuff he'd seen when they'd rescued Gritt from the dungeons. Goo.

He found Pa's mate Bruzer stirring a large clay pot that sat in one of the cracks in the floor. The pot was half-full of crushed rock, and trickles of metal glinted among the stone. The smoke stung his eyes.

'How do, youngster,' said Bruzer. 'What brings you here?'

'A favour,' said Muncle. 'It won't take a moment. I just need some of your Goo.'

'A lot of people have been asking for Goo since firewood got more expensive, but we're not giving it away. We need it ourselves.'

'Oh, I only want a spoonful ... to ... er ... show Biblos. He can't get down here himself and he wants to know what it's like.'

'Ah, for *Biblos*. Then of course you can have some. Always happy to help him. He did a wonderful job frightening away the Smallings with his forest fire idea.'

'Yes, he did, didn't he?' Muncle pulled the pot out of his bag.

'His Wiseness's ideas are far too clever for me.' Bruzer laughed again. 'Too clever for you as well, I'll bet.'

'Er, yes,' said Muncle, as Bruzer ladled Goo into the pot. 'Much too clever.' He wondered if anyone would ever believe they were *his* ideas.

Holding the pot carefully by the handles, he carried it home. Gritt was back from school, and Pa had got up. Piglitt had woken too, and Flubb was trying to catch her. Piglitt could run faster than Flubb could crawl, and Flubb chose the very moment Muncle came in through the door to get to her feet for the first time and try to run. Ma dived to catch her before she fell, and Pa and Gritt roared with laughter as Ma, Flubb and Piglitt ended up in a heap together on the floor.

Muncle slipped quickly into his bedroom. He hid the pot in a cubby-hole in the wall, so he didn't have to answer any awkward questions about it. He didn't want to frighten anyone with volcano warnings till he was absolutely sure there was something to worry about.

Goo - handle with care!

Chapter ten

Ma had insisted on giving Muncle another dose of Willow Juice at bedtime, so he slept deeply and didn't wake until voices in the kitchen disturbed him. He looked over at the cubby hole. The pot was no longer glowing orange. He shot out of bed for a closer look.

The Goo had gone. In its place was a grey pebble.

He threw his curtain aside and burst into the kitchen.

'Gritt, have you been in my room?'

Gritt was already on his second helping of fungus porridge.

'No, of course I haven't. I couldn't *get* into your room – it's too small.'

All the family slept in holes in the kitchen walls, but Muncle's was much smaller than the others, only just big enough for his bracken mattress.

Muncle ran his hands through his tangled hair. 'Well, *someone* must have,' he muttered to himself.

Ma looked at him anxiously. 'What's the matter?' she said.

'Nothing, Ma. It's just Wise Man stuff.' He went back into his room, and put the pebble in his pocket. It was rather rough and not nearly as heavy as he'd expected. Then he squeezed the empty pot into his bag – he was going to have to get some more Goo but there wasn't enough time before he met Emily. If he didn't turn up she'd just go home and he might never see her again.

Gritt waited impatiently while Muncle ate his breakfast. 'I'm going to be very late if I walk at your speed,' he said. 'Do you want me to carry you?'

'*No!*' said Muncle. 'Thank you,' he added. He knew Gritt was just trying to be helpful. It had been all right getting a lift from his younger brother when they were out hunting and there'd been no-one else around to see them, but he'd be laughed at if he did it in the middle of the town.

Muncle left most of his breakfast and hurried to his den. Emily wasn't there.

Flimflams. If he'd known she was going to be late he could have gone and got some more Goo after all. But there was really no point in her coming at all, now he'd got nothing to show her. If he went to meet her he could save her the long climb up through the forest.

There had been no path beside the stream when he'd first gone down to the town for a look at Smallings, but since then a thin track had been worn through the plants that grew along the bank. Muncle walked for some time before he caught a glimpse of yellow hair and sparkly pink bag between the trees.

'Sorry I'm late,' puffed Emily. 'I came straight after breakfast, but I don't get up very early in the holidays. Muncle, what are you doing right down here? People on my street might see you.'

'I wanted to stop you coming any further. I haven't got the Goo.'

'Oh.'

'Well, I *got* it, but Gritt stole it in the night. He says it wasn't him, but it must have been. Flubb couldn't have reached it. He left a stone in its place, which is just the sort of trick Gritt likes to play.'

'A stone? What sort of stone?'

Muncle pulled the grey pebble out of his pocket.

Emily pulled a grey pebble out of her bag. 'Snap!' she said.

'What?'

'It's a game we play, where you say "Snap" if you turn up two cards with the same picture on them.'

'I see,' said Muncle, though he didn't see at all.

'I just mean your stone is the same as my stone.'

Muncle peered at Emily's stone. It was a different shape from his, but it was grey and had the same rough surface, pitted with tiny holes.

'Where did you get yours?' he asked.

'From our bathroom. Look.' She pulled the volcano book out of her bag and turned to a picture – of a rough grey stone pitted with tiny holes. 'Pumice,' she said. 'We use it to get our hands clean if they're really dirty, like this.'

She knelt down beside the stream, dipped her hands in the water and rubbed them with her stone. 'D'you want a go?'

Muncle rubbed water on to his grimy hands with his own stone. He watched as they became paler and smoother. In his surprise he let the stone slip from his fingers. But instead of sinking, it bobbed away, floating down the stream. Emily ran and caught it.

'We've always had a pumice-stone in our bathroom,' she said, 'but I didn't know where it came from until I read more of my book last night.'

'But it can't be stone if it floats. Stones are heavy. What is it? Where did Gritt find it?'

'Muncle, Gritt didn't steal your Goo. That stone *is* your Goo. Pumice comes from volcanoes. It's what lava turns into when it cools down. All those little holes are where air got trapped when it was bubbling hot. It's the air trapped inside that makes it light enough to float.'

This was terrible news.

Muncle leaned against a tree trunk. He felt quite faint. 'So our Goo is your lava,' he said unhappily, 'and Mount Grumble really is going to blow up.'

Emily sat down beside him. She took off her strappy open shoes and splashed her feet in the stream. 'It's still only a Yellow Alert,' she said. 'You still might have time to get your dragons flying.'

Only *might*!

Muncle gulped. 'We haven't even stopped clipping the dragons' wings yet. It could take ages for them to heal. And nobody will believe me if I tell them we've got to get out. Even Biblos doesn't believe Mount Grumble's a volcano.'

He shut his eyes, rubbed the donkey badge on his chain and muttered to himself.

'What are you doing?' said Emily.

'Asking the Wonder Donkey to work a wonder and save us from the volcano.'

'Oh. Er ... is that what Wonder Donkeys do?'

'Yes.' Muncle heaved a huge sigh. 'But I'm afraid it probably has to be a real Wonder Donkey, not just a picture of one. I'm going to have to do this on my own.' He got to his feet.

'Good luck,' Emily said as she squeezed her wet feet back into her shoes.

It wasn't until he was halfway home that he realised his head was so full of worry that he hadn't even said goodbye.

'Just in time for dinner.' Biblos waved a rib-bone as Muncle walked into the museum. 'Are you happy to share my braised badger, or do you want to go to MuckGristle's and choose your own dinner?'

'Badger's one of my favourites. Thanks.' Muncle gnawed a rib. 'Biblos, what do you think this is?' He pulled his grey pebble out of his pocket.

Biblos peered at it. 'It's a stone,' he said.

'It's not an *ordinary* stone, though, is it?'

Biblos picked it up and brought it so close to his eyes that it bumped into his nose.

'Looks ordinary enough to me,' he said, 'though I can't see as well as I used to.'

'But you can *feel* it, can't you? You can tell that it's light and rough?'

'Oh, there's lots of stone around that's light and rough. The Crater floor is made of this sort of stone.'

'It is?' Muncle had never noticed, but then he'd never been that interested in stone before. 'Biblos, do you realise what this stone *is*?'

Biblos shrugged and went back to his dinner. 'It's just stone,' he said.

'No, it's *Goo*.'

Biblos spluttered, showering Muncle with half-chewed badger. 'Muncle, a clever chap like you must know that Goo is orange. And hot. And sticky.'

'This pebble was orange and hot and sticky when it came out of the ground yesterday. When it cooled down it went grey and hard.'

'Really? That's fascinating. Have another rib.'

'But don't you see what this *means*? Biblos, a long time ago the Crater must have been full of Goo. It proves that what Emily told us was true. There really *are* things called volcanoes, and Mount Grumble really *is* one.'

'The Smalling girl? Told us the truth? Well I'm blowed. I didn't know Smallings ever did that.'

'But aren't you worried?' said Muncle, wondering if the old man had heard him properly. 'MOUNT GRUMBLE IS A VOLCANO!'

'*Was*,' Biblos mumbled round a mouthful of badger. 'You said "a long time ago", Muncle. Mount Grumble *was* a volcano. Nothing to worry about nowadays.'

Muncle tried again. 'Biblos, where was the Goo when you were a boy?'

'Oh, there wasn't any. No. It's quite a recent thing. Splendid, isn't it?'

Muncle shuddered. 'Haven't you ever wondered why?'

'Not my job,' Biblos said, mildly. 'I only think about the things the King asks me to think about.'

'But the Wise Man is wiser than the King. He should think about things that the King doesn't realise need thinking about.'

Biblos's straggly grey eyebrows drew together in a frown. 'Sorry, Muncle. You've lost me now. There were

If only they
would listen
to the
Wise Minikin.

too many "things" and "thinks" in what you just said.'

Muncle took a deep breath. 'Biblos, Mount Grumble is getting hotter. Everyone says so. And it's getting hotter because there's more Goo, and when there gets to be *enough* Goo, Mount Grumble will blow up!'

Biblos chuckled. 'That wouldn't be *enough* Goo, Muncle. It would be too much.'

'Biblos, this is SERIOUS. We need to be ready to get away quickly.'

'What, you and me?'

'Everyone. The whole town.'

'Impossible.' Biblos leaned back in his rocking chair and put his feet on the table. 'We couldn't all leave the town without the Smallings seeing us. And we can't run faster than their magic carts.'

'We won't be running. We'll be flying. We've got to stop clipping dragons' wings, Biblos, so they can all fly like Snarg.'

'*Flying?*' Biblos giggled. 'Think of the chaos,' he said. 'Flying dragons everywhere, getting hotter and stronger with all that sun. Think of the accidents, dragons crashing into each other, people falling off. Oh, that's a good joke, Muncle.'

'It's not a *joke*,' Muncle said desperately. 'If we don't fly we'll blow up!'

'Of course we won't,' said Biblos. 'Muncle, you're doing too much thinking and that isn't wise at all. The King won't like it if you keep coming up with crazy ideas. Now, if you could just bring me the blanket out of the chest over there ... and the cushion ...'

Within seconds Biblos had dozed off.

Muncle was very upset. He was the only giant who knew Mount Grumble was in terrible danger. And he couldn't do anything about it until after tomorrow's Victory Feast. Nobody was listening to him – and that wouldn't change until the King made him Wise Man in front of everyone.

Muncle had to keep quiet about volcanoes until then. If the King thought he was crazy and changed his mind, they'd all be roasted alive!

Scrape this up for a tasty snack.

Chapter eleven

It was the morning of the Victory Feast. Ma was rubbing bramble juice on to Flubb's cheeks to give them a healthy purple glow, and had coloured every one of her warts with some pretty yellow Goo-dust. From a distance her round face looked as yellow as the rising sun. Pa was doing last minute muscle-building exercises, lifting Ma's water pot above his head. Muncle had sent Gritt out early to take Piglitt to the Princess, even though it was a holiday.

Muncle would have taken Piglitt himself, but he wasn't dressed yet. He itched all over and was busy rubbing himself with Ma's Mustard Mend ointment. Last night Ma had patched and darned his ragged, holey clothes so that he would look smart when he was introduced as the new Wise Man. But he only had one set, so he'd had to sleep with nothing on, and the creepy crawlies that lived in his bracken mattress had nibbled him from head to heels. He pulled the clothes on over the sticky ointment and slipped the Wise Man's Chain under his jerkin, hoping the King would never get to see that it was held together by string.

At last they were ready. Draggly had already had his medicine and gone back to sleep, his feet covered in Mustard Mend and bandaged to stop him licking it off. He would be all right on his own till they got back.

They were in good time, but the Crater was already busy. The Smash-a-Smalling side show was doing a roaring trade. The 'Smalling' – made of string-cloth – was already losing its dried-grass stuffing.

The best seats were in the grandstand and, thanks to Puglug's nugget, the Troggs were able to afford them for the first time ever. As they climbed up to take their places a huge shadow fell over them all. Everyone ducked.

'Muncle,' Ma cried, 'it's your flying dragon!'

The crowd gasped in amazement. Everyone knew by now that there was a dragon flying free, but most of them had never seen it.

Muncle was amazed too. Why would Snarg come

into the Crater, without even being asked to?

Snarg flew up and swooped down again several times, each time getting closer to the Troggs.

On the final swoop he seized Muncle by his breeches belt and flew off with him.

The crowd gasped in horror.

'Muncle!' screamed Ma, Pa and Gritt.

'Mumble!' screamed Flubb.

'It's all right!' Muncle yelled. 'Don't worry! Snarg won't hurt me.' But he didn't know if they could hear him. Bent double, he swung backwards and forwards from the dragon's claws. 'What is it, Snarg?' he wheezed. 'Where are we going? Why do you need me? Are you hurt again? Ill?'

But Snarg was flying like a dragon in the best of health. He cleared the top of Mount Grumble, glided down over the tree tops and dived into the clearing beside Muncle's den. He hovered just above the ground and let go, giving Muncle room to somersault and land on his feet.

'Interesting ride, Snarg,' said Muncle, as he dusted himself off, 'but I didn't actually want to come here today. I've got to be in the Crater for my Wise Man's

Dragon-flying –
it's the only
way to travel.

ceremony.' He climbed on to the dragon's back, grabbed the dragon flute hanging on its chain round his neck, and blew 'Up Up Up'.

Snarg lay down.

Muncle was just wondering if he was going to have to get off and walk home when he heard a strange shuffling noise from inside the hut.

Puzzled, he slid off Snarg's back. But before he could reach the door it swung open and the thing that was making the noise stepped carefully over the threshold.

Muncle gasped.

The thing was brown all over and walked on two legs, like a giant or a Smalling, though rather awkwardly, because it had no arms. It was the strangest creature he had ever seen. But its long nose and ears were unmistakable.

Muncle fell to his knees and bowed down before it.

It was a Wonder Donkey.

'Get up, Muncle,' said the Wonder Donkey, in a muffled voice that sounded like a giggle.

It knew his name! Muncle didn't dare *look* up, let alone get up.

The creature shuffled over to him. 'Don't you

recognise me?'

'Of course I do.' Muncle whispered, his eyes fixed on the ground. 'You're a Wonder Donkey.'

'Oh, you are funny! Look at me properly.'

Slowly Muncle raised his head. He felt his heart stand still with shock as the donkey's head lifted off its shoulders – and a smaller head appeared underneath.

'*Emily?*' Muncle's heart started to beat again and he scrambled to his feet.

'Did you really think I was a Wonder Donkey?' she asked.

'Well, yes,' Muncle admitted. 'I mean, it's an easy mistake to make. I wasn't expecting to find you here, and I've never seen a Wonder Donkey before – nobody has.'

'It's a horse really, just the front end. When I wore it in my school play my friend was the back legs. I stuffed two old socks and sewed them on to the ears to make them longer.'

Snarg looked from Emily's head to the donkey's head. He seemed confused.

Emily patted him. 'Well done, Snarg! You brilliant dragon.'

It took Muncle a few moments to work out what she meant. 'You mean ... you mean you *sent* Snarg to get me?'

'Well, I *hoped* that was what I'd done. I blew the signal I'd heard you use for "Come Here" on your old flute, and when he came, I blew "Up Up Up". But I didn't know if he'd understand that I wanted him to fetch you, and I didn't know whether he could find you even if he *did* understand.'

The knot of fear was back in Muncle's belly. '*Why* did you send for me?' he asked.

'I thought if you really couldn't make the giants understand the danger, perhaps I could help you by bringing a Wonder Donkey costume for you to wear.'

'Well, it fooled me, all right,' said Muncle. 'But I'm afraid it'll be too small.'

'Oh.' Emily looked crestfallen. 'I hadn't thought of that.' She chewed her bottom lip. 'But Muncle, you have to do something. The alert's changed to Amber.'

Muncle sat down hurriedly on the tree trunk. 'How soon before it changes to Red?'

Emily sat down beside him. 'They're not sure yet, but it could be just a few days. Mum and Dad are packing so that we're ready to move to my grandma's the minute we're told to leave.'

'*Days*? Then we can't escape, Emily. We haven't even stopped clipping the dragons' wings yet. They'll never heal in time.'

'I've thought of that.' Emily wriggled her arms out of the neck of the donkey suit, and dived back into the hut. She came out carrying a shopping bag full of small packets. She opened one, took out a little pink strip and gave it to Muncle.

'What is it?'

'A sticking plaster.'

'Sticky what?'

'Plaster. We use them to hold the sides of a cut together until it's healed.'

Muncle turned the strip this way and that, then handed it back. 'But it isn't sticky,' he said.

Emily showed him how to peel away a layer of paper. Underneath it the strip was really, really sticky.

'Oh! You mean we can stick the dragons' wings back together and they'll be able to fly straight away?' Muncle gave Emily an enormous hug and they both fell backwards off the tree trunk.

'Ouch, Muncle!'

'Sorry, but that's a real Wonder Donkey wonder!'

'I can't promise it will work,' Emily said anxiously. 'The plasters may not stick to dragon scales. And even if they do, they may not be strong enough to stay stuck when the dragons try to fly.'

'Oh.'

'But you have to try. And if the plasters don't work you could always stitch the dragons' wings.'

'Stitch?' Muncle thought this must be one of those words that meant something different in Smalling-speak. Stitching was something Ma did in knitting and sewing.

'Yes, I once fell over and got a really deep cut on my forehead and a doctor at the hospital put three stitches in it with a special needle and thread.'

She *did* mean sewing stitches! Muncle peered at her forehead.

'Oh, the stitches aren't there now.' Emily brushed her fringe aside to show a faint line on her skin. 'A nurse took them out again when the cut had healed.'

Muncle wasn't sure how the dragons would feel about having needles stuck in their wings, but the stickies sounded perfect.

'Thank you, *thank* you, Emily.' Muncle picked up the bag. 'Can you get more of these stickies if we need them?'

Emily shook her head. 'I've used up all my pocket money,' she said.

'You *paid* for them? With your own nugglins? Emily, that's so ...' Muncle felt a sudden warm glow in his belly where the knot of fear had been. He opened his arms wide.

'Don't hug me again!' Emily ducked out of the way hurriedly. 'It's all right, I wasn't saving up for anything special. And I think saving giants and dragons is pretty special anyway. More special than a new computer game.'

'You're right, Emily. Saving giants and dragons *is* special.' Muncle leapt up. 'I'll go home and get people to start sticking dragon wings together ...' He hesitated. 'Except they won't want to do it today. Everyone's at the Feast.'

'Are you having another party? So soon after the King's Birthday?'

Muncle felt too embarrassed to admit that they were celebrating frightening the Smallings away.

'It's for the King to announce that I'm the new Wise Man,' he said. 'I must get back—'

He stopped. He looked at the donkey suit, and he

looked at Emily.

'Come with me, Emily.'

'*What*?'

'It was your idea to dress up as a Wonder Donkey. Come and do it now.'

Emily looked terrified. ' I really meant you to dress up, not me. I don't dare, Muncle. Not today, anyway. Not at a party. It'd be too much like the King's Birthday, after I was kidnapped.'

'But Emily, it has to be today. There's a danger the King might not make me Wise Man after all, what with me being so small and only just out of school. But having a Wonder Donkey would make all the difference. It would make me the greatest Wise Man ever.'

'Muncle—'

'You wouldn't have to get near any full-sized giants. We needn't even land.'

'*Land*? You mean you want me to fly in on *Snarg*?'

'Well of course I do,' said Muncle. 'That's the whole point. If people see a Wonder Donkey flying, they'll all want to try it. And then we might just have a chance of escaping Mount Grumble before it blows.'

chapter twelve

They glided over the forest. Emily, stiff with fear, was safely wedged between Muncle and Snarg's collar.

'Isn't it splendid?' said Muncle.

'What?'

'The view.'

'I don't know,' squeaked Emily. 'I've got my eyes shut.'

Muncle remembered his own first flight. 'You'll be fine once you get used to it,' he said. 'We'll fly around a bit for practice before we go into the Crater.'

They circled above the mountain top. Little by little, Muncle felt Emily relax.

'It's all right,' she said after a while. 'I've got my eyes open now. But ...' she sniffed. 'Euugh! What's that stink?'

'Don't you like it?' said Muncle. 'It's just the Farts competition.'

'*What*?'

'Wait a moment, that can't be right. It's not Burps and Farts today.'

'That's a rotten cabbage smell,' Emily gasped. 'That's sulphur – another of the warning signs.'

'Flimflams!'

'Muncle ...' Emily began, but they were in sight of the crowd now and there was no time for any more questions.

They swooped into the Crater. Below them, half the crowd was clapping as Bruzer Biffit lifted a huge lump of iron in the Most Massive Muscles Competition. Pa was on the stage waiting his turn, but he was looking at the sky rather than the stage. The other half of the crowd, including the rest of the Trogg family, was also anxiously watching the sky.

As Snarg came into view, with Muncle no longer in his claws but sitting on his back, Ma leapt to her feet screaming with relief. A huge cheer went up. Startled, Bruzer dropped the lump of iron on his toes, his yelp of pain echoing all around the Crater. The clapping and cheering was replaced by a sudden stunned silence as

Snarg came closer and everyone could see that Muncle was not alone.

Biblos, who was judging the competition, shuffled to the front of the stage and peered up. Above him, King Thortless leapt off his throne and leaned over the palace balcony for a closer look. Puglug, with Piglitt clasped in her arms, stood up on her throne for a better view. The little pig was wearing a sheepskin robe and a tiny golden crown.

'Sit down, both of you!' Queen Fattipat hissed at her husband and daughter as Muncle flew past. 'You're behaving in a most undignified and unroyal manner.'

Neither of them took any notice.

Muncle persuaded Snarg to land high up on the flagpole that stuck out from the palace roof, where he seemed to feel safe.

'What is it?' King Thortless called down to the stage. 'Tell me what it is, Biblos.'

Biblos didn't hear him – he had dropped his ear trumpet as he fell to his knees and bowed his face to the floor.

But the King still got his answer.

'I know what it is!' squealed Princess Puglug, jumping up and down on her throne and nearly

dropping Piglitt in her excitement. 'It's a Wonder Donkey!'

The colour drained from the King's face until it was as pale as his sheepskin robes. 'Thrumbling thrimthrams,' he muttered, throwing himself hastily to the floor. His crown flew over the balcony railings and landed on top of Pa's head on the stage below.

'OUCH!' Pa took the crown off to see what had hit him, grinned broadly – showing more gaps than teeth – and put it on again.

The Wonder Donkey made a funny noise as Emily tried not to giggle, but the giants were too busy falling to their knees and bowing down to notice.

'Say something,' Muncle whispered to Emily urgently. '*Talk* to them.'

'EE-AW!' Emily shouted loudly.

Muncle nearly jumped out of his skin. 'What does that mean?' he hissed.

'Well, I can't talk to them,' Emily hissed back. 'I sound like a Smalling. That's the noise donkeys make.'

'Really? Well, good idea. You make donkey noises and I'll pretend to translate them into giant-speak.'

'EE-AW! EE-AW!' Emily opened and shut the donkey's mouth from the inside so it really looked as if

Bow down before
the wonder of the
Wonder Donkey.

the donkey was talking.

'Citizens of Mount Grumble!' Muncle yelled.

No-one could hear his little voice and, since they were all bowed down, no-one even saw that the tiny figure on the dragon was trying to say something. No-one except Puglug, who was much too interested in looking up at the Wonder Donkey on the flagpole to bother about bowing down.

'Citizens of Mount Grumble!' Puglug shouted helpfully. Her voice was enormous. She'd have made a good Town Crier if she hadn't been so royal. She looked up at Muncle, waiting for more.

'The Wonder Donkey wants you to go back to your seats and listen to what it has to say,' Muncle shouted, and Puglug repeated the message ten times louder.

Everyone picked themselves up and settled down. Pa, still wearing the King's crown, found Biblos's ear-trumpet and helped the old man to his feet.

'EE-AW,' shouted Emily. 'EE-AW, EE-AW, EE-AW!'

'What's it saying?' Puglug called.

'Look after your dragons, giants of Mount Grumble,' yelled Muncle, searching for suitably impressive words, 'for they are noble beasts who will serve you well.'

'Look after your dragons!' boomed Puglug.

Muncle prodded Emily.

'EE-AW, EE-AW!'

'Free them from their cages, feed them on sunshine, mend their wings and ...'

'Free them, feed them, mend their wings,' yelled Puglug.

'EE-AW, EE-AW, EE-AW!'

'... learn to ride them so that you can all travel through the skies the way Wonder Donkeys travel.'

'And ride them through the skies!' Puglug leapt up and down on her throne in excitement.

Now a gasp went up and the giants, who'd been sitting in stunned silence, at last started talking to one another. The King, bald and surprisingly short without his crown, stomped down the stairs from the balcony. He marched across the stage to Biblos.

'What's going on?' whispered Emily.

'I don't know,' Muncle whispered back. 'But the King's trying to say something.'

'May I have the Wonder Donkey's permission to speak?' the King called up to them nervously.

'That's what the Wonder Donkey is waiting for,' said Muncle.

'Oh – thank you very much.' The King took a deep breath. 'People of Mount Grumble,' he began, in a tiny voice.

Throughout the Crater the chattering went on. The King's voice was no louder than Muncle's. The Town Crier gave the gong an almighty whack.

BOIOIOING!

Immediately the crowd stopped chattering.

'Pray silence for His Enormity King Thortless the Thirteenth!' announced the Town Crier, in a voice nearly as loud as the gong itself.

The crowd looked expectantly at the stage.

King Thortless cleared his throat. 'People of Mount Grumble,' he began again, 'today is not just the day on which we celebrate our victory over the Smallings ...'

'*What*?' Emily shuddered.

'Sorry.' Muncle gave her a little squeeze, remembering just in time to make it a gentle one. 'I should have told you. We planned this party when we thought you'd all run away.'

Biblos muttered something in the King's ear and the King went on: '... today is also the day on which we all say a big "thank you" to the wise giant who made that victory possible.'

'Hooray!' shouted voices in the crowd. 'Good old Biblos!' Deafening clapping broke out.

BOIOIOING! The Town Crier had to hit his gong again.

'Not Biblos,' said the King, 'who is retiring as Wise Man, but the only citizen who has ever brought a Wonder Donkey into our town. I present to you my new Wise Minik ... Wise Man, er ...' He stuttered to a halt and turned to Biblos for advice.

Pa beat Biblos to it. 'Muncle Trogg!' he shouted, tossing the King's crown in the air.

'Ah, yes. That's it. I present to you all my new Wise Man, Muncle Trogg.'

The King's announcement was greeted by total silence.

Then Biblos waved his ear trumpet and drummed loudly on the stage with his stick. 'Hurrah!' he shouted. 'Hurrah for Wise Man Muncle and the Flying Wonder Donkey!'

Now the giants understood. The old Wise Man supported the King's strange choice of new Wise Man. It wasn't a mistake.

In the grandstand Ma and Gritt leapt to their feet and started to clap.

'Hurrah!' Pa waved the King's crown in the air and led the cheering from the stage.

'Hurrah!' the crowd shouted back, and they clapped loudly and stamped till the Crater rumbled and the grandstands nearly fell down. Pa plonked the crown back on the King's head and shook his hand so hard that the King fell over.

'Can we go, now he's made you Wise Man?' asked Emily. 'This donkey head is rather heavy.'

'Of course. Here we go.'

They took off from the flagpole and flew one last lap of the Crater before heading back to the clearing.

'Emily,' said Muncle, as they flew over the forest, 'how come you know what sort of noise donkeys make?'

'Because I've heard them, of course.'

Muncle nearly fell off Snarg's back. 'You've heard a real live donkey? Have you seen one too?'

Emily laughed. 'I've even ridden on one – there are quite a few where my grandma lives.'

'Your grandma lives in Back of Beyond?'

Emily laughed again. 'No, of course not. Muncle, the donkeys I know are just ordinary ones. I haven't ridden on a *Wonder* Donkey.'

'Oh,' said Muncle as they landed in the clearing. 'I thought all donkeys were Wonder Donkeys.'

'I don't think so,' said Emily. 'But they are all very sweet and gentle.'

Muncle helped her out of the donkey suit and she collected her pink sparkly bag from the hut.

'So,' she said, 'what do we do now?'

'I start mending dragons,' said Muncle, 'and you go back to being a Smalling.'

'But what if I have to tell you we've got a Red Alert? I know I can find you at the museum, but I don't know how to get into Mount Grumble and find my way to the Crater. I might be able to call Snarg, but I couldn't fly him by myself.'

'You'd have to follow that track.' Muncle pointed. 'It leads to a broken gate in the mountainside. Inside you turn right and keep going till you get to the Crater.'

'Turn right and keep going,' Emily spoke slowly as if trying to fix it in her memory.

'If there's a Red Alert you mustn't come, though,' said Muncle. 'It'll be much too dangerous and you'll be leaving town.'

They stood and looked anxiously at each other for a long time.

'Well, I suppose this is goodbye, then,' Emily said at last.

Muncle swallowed hard. 'Thank you so much for coming with me, Emily,' he said, remembering just in time not to hurt her with one of his too-strong hugs. 'I'm not sure I'd be Wise Man now if the King hadn't seen me with the Wonder Donkey.'

'EE-AW,' said Emily with a rather sad smile. 'I'm glad I could help.' She reached out and bravely gave Snarg a quick pat on the leg. 'Goodbye, Snarg. I hope I'll get another chance to ride you one day.'

Snarg puffed out a smoke ring from each nostril.

'He hopes so too,' said Muncle.

He watched Emily disappear into the forest, then he gave Snarg a *proper* pat, a good slap hard enough for him to feel through his scales. 'Off you go, boy,' he said, 'to wherever it is you're living now. I'll see you again soon.'

He blew his new signal for 'Take Off', picked up Emily's shopping bag of stickies, and set off for home on foot. That way he could slip into the Crater unnoticed.

*

But he didn't go unnoticed at all.

For the first time in his life he didn't have to fight his way between legs and dodge trampling feet. The crowd parted to let him through. A few people even bowed down to him, even though he no longer had the Wonder Donkey with him. When he knocked on the palace door he was received like an honoured guest.

Biblos and the King were in the Throne Chamber, a splendid room Muncle had never seen before. The throne itself was bigger than Muncle's whole bedroom, but all Muncle could see were its dragon-claw feet and the dragon-head armrests. The rest of it was buried under piles of moss-filled cushions, layers of reed-cloth rugs and the bulk of King Thortless himself. Biblos struggled to get out of his rather-less-splendid chair as the footman showed Muncle in.

'Where is it?' the King asked. 'Where's the Wonder Donkey?'

Muncle was just about to make something up when he remembered the legend – Wonder Donkeys came from Back of Beyond.

'Gone home,' he said. If anything would tempt people to fly to Back of Beyond it would be to see the home of the Wonder Donkey.

'But I wanted it to live in my palace.' The King sounded disappointed.

'Muncle,' said Biblos, 'you've never been to Back of Beyond, so how did you find it?'

'I didn't. It found me. It sent Snarg to fetch me because it wanted to tell us to fly.'

'Amazing!' Biblos bent down and shook him solemnly by the hand. 'Muncle, you are indeed the Wise Man that Mount Grumble has been waiting for ever since the Smallings got magic. The first Wise Man to be friends with a Wonder Donkey.'

The King frowned. 'But *why* does the Wonder Donkey want us to fly?' he said. 'Giants have never flown before.'

'It told me we *have* flown before, Your Enormity, a very long time ago, before there were any Smallings.'

'You mean it was how we lived in the good old days, when giants ruled the world from Back of Beyond? Oh, now I understand. It wants us to rule the world again, and it's come to help us!'

Biblos shook his head. 'I'm afraid I'm much too old to learn dragon-riding,' he said sadly.

'Don't worry.' The King slapped Biblos on the shoulder, nearly knocking him over. 'Now that we have a Wise Minikin with a Wonder Donkey to grant all our wishes, we'll never need to worry about anything ever again.'

His Enormity
King Thortless

Chapter thirteen

The grandstands, thick with a new layer of dust, were being taken down by a team of sleepy workmen as Muncle hurried through the Crater next morning. The Victory Feast had turned into a Wonder Donkey Feast and gone on long past his bed-time.

Most of the stall-holders weren't at work yet, but one was already doing a roaring trade: the hat-maker. She had been up all night knitting donkey-ears to commemorate the Wonder Donkey's visit and there was a huge crowd around her stall, bowing to each other and happily saying 'Ee-Aw!' as they tied their ears on to their heads.

Muncle cast a worried look at the smoke cloud above the mountain as he hurried past the stalls. It looked a lot thicker than usual. All the more reason to get the dragons mended as quickly as possible.

When he got to the museum he found a Guardsman dozing on the door, Biblos still in his nightshirt, and Puglug wide awake.

'The Wonder Donkey,' she said, bouncing up and down with excitement. 'I want a lesson about the Wonder Donkey!'

'Me too!' Biblos stifled a yawn.

'I'm afraid I can't teach you much,' said Muncle, 'because I don't know much myself. The Wonder Donkey is also a *Secret* Donkey.'

'Aowww, you're the Wise Man,' whined Puglug. 'You must know *something*.'

'I know it lives in Back of Beyond. Would you like a lesson about that?'

'No. I know about Back of Beyond. I did it last year. I want to know how the Wonder Donkey works its wonders.'

'Right. Well, in that case today's lesson is How To Mend Cuts.' Muncle climbed on to a stool and put Emily's shopping bag on the table.

'*Wonders*!' Puglug banged her fists on the table.

'As I said, today's lesson is How To Mend Cuts – using wonders.'

'Oh.' Puglug calmed down. 'Not cobwebs?' She pulled up the hem of her moleskin skirt to reveal a gash in her knee, filled with a mass of sticky threads.

'Not cobwebs.' Muncle tipped the contents of the bag on to the table. 'Look. Each of these pink stickies is a little wonder.'

He pulled off the backing paper and put one of the stickies on Puglug's cut.

'Nice,' she said, admiring the tiny pink patch on her large grey knee, 'that's pretty. I want a pink wonder on the other knee too, and on my elbows and my nose.' She jumped up, grabbing a handful of the precious stickies. 'I'm going to show Ma straight away.'

'No!' said Muncle. 'They're for mending dragons' wings, so they can fly. That's why the Wonder Donkey gave me them.'

'Oooh, *are* they?' Puglug's eyes opened wide and she grabbed another handful. 'Thank you, Wonder Donkey!'

Muncle bundled the rest of the stickies back into the bag as Puglug marched out, calling for her guard.

'Well, if today's lesson is over already,' he said, 'I'd better go and start on the dragons.' He jumped down off the stool.

'Muncle ...' Biblos began.

'Yes?'

'Er ... did the Wonder Donkey say why it wanted us to start flying? Did it mention anything about ... *Goo*?'

Muncle looked into Biblos's worried grey eyes and realised that the old man was frightened – frightened that Mount Grumble might really be a volcano after all, and frightened that he was too old to fly to safety if it blew up.

'No,' he said hurriedly. 'It just wants us to fly because it's an old skill we should never have lost.'

Biblos heaved a huge sigh and sank back into his rocking chair. 'Phew. You go and start mending wings, then. I can't wait to see all the dragons flying – just like Snarg.'

Muncle ran all the way to the King's Guard Barracks. There were more dragons here than anywhere else, and they were better trained too, so they would get the knack of flying fastest. These were the ones to mend first.

Muncle knocked on the Barracks door. The Captain opened it himself. His eyes were only half open and his purple tunic was buttoned up in the wrong holes. He yawned, noticed the Wise Man's Chain, and hurriedly pulled himself together.

'Er … good morning Your Wiseness Wise Minikin … I'm … er … sorry I picked you up by the scruff of the neck the other day,' he said with an awkward bow.

What a difference it made having a Wonder Donkey as your best friend!

'Don't worry about it,' said Muncle. 'Just follow the Wonder Donkey's orders now, please, and bring the Dragon Division out into the Crater.'

'Wonder Donkey's orders!' The Captain sprinted into the Barracks and, after a lot of shouting, he hauled Pompom, his magnificent Purple Noble dragon, into the Crater, followed by fifty more sleepy, untidy soldiers, each leading a Common Green or Common Red. They drew up in battle order, five rows of ten.

'Splendid, aren't they?' said the Captain, proudly.

'Very handsome,' agreed Muncle.

'You're allowed a Purple Noble too, you know, now you're Wise Minikin.'

For a moment Muncle imagined how brilliant a Purple Noble would look with sunlight pouring down on its outstretched wings. Then he felt guilty. Snarg had helped him when life had been difficult, and he would be loyal to Snarg for ever.

'My Dragon Division are already expert dragon handlers,' the Captain said. 'They'll be natural dragon-riders – you won't have to teach them a thing.'

'I'm sure,' said Muncle, 'but first we're going to mend the dragons' wings so they can fly. Make your dragons lie down, please.'

Fifty-one men blew the command on their dragon flutes.

Only fifty dragons lay down.

The Captain's face turned as purple as his dragon. 'Er ... my flute doesn't seem to be working,' he muttered.

Muncle blew 'Lie Down' on his own dragon flute. The Captain's dragon lowered its head, peered into Muncle's tiny eyes and sniffed him. Then it lay down. The Captain's face turned an interesting shade of even darker purple.

Guess who's not that keen on flying lessons?

'Now,' Muncle said, turning back to the soldiers, 'watch this carefully, everybody. Captain, ask your dragon to spread his wings, please.'

The Captain tilted back his helmet so he could scratch his head. 'But there isn't a signal for that,' he said.

Muncle thought about this. 'Maybe you could try tickling him?'

The Captain tickled his dragon. It blew two little smoke rings, made a noise that sounded like a chuckle and wriggled his wings. Muncle grabbed hold of the left one.

'Hold the cut together, please, Captain,' he said. Dipping into the shopping bag, he pulled out a sticky and plonked it on the dragon's wing.

The tiny pink patch looked even sillier on the vast wing than it had done on Puglug's chubby grey knee. Muncle lost count of the number of stickies he had to use as he patched up both wings. But it worked. The dragon flapped its outstretched wings and looked at them, as if puzzled to see them moving.

Muncle turned to the soldiers again. 'Now I want you all to mend your dragons in the same way.' He looked into the bag. It wasn't bulging any more. He'd already used half the stickies – on just *one* dragon. How was he going to fix the rest? 'Tomorrow,' he said. 'We'll mend the rest of your dragons *tomorrow*.'

Once the Captain had led the Dragon Division back to their stables, Muncle walked slowly round the Crater, wondering how on earth he was going to solve his latest problem by tomorrow. There just weren't enough stickies for all the dragons in Mount Grumble. Emily had suggested sewing the wings, but if clipping wings hurt the dragons – and he was sure it did – then sticking needles in them was going to hurt too. He was lost in thought when a figure limped out of the shadows, seized him by his Chain, and twisted it round his throat.

'I'm sorry, Titan,' Muncle croaked, 'but I really can't help to get you back into the King's Guard.'

'Of course *you* can't, you miserable little minikin,' said Titan Bulge, 'but your Wonder Donkey can work wonders.' He twisted the Chain tighter. 'Or can it? If it could, it would have turned you into a proper giant by now, wouldn't it?'

This was really alarming. Titan clearly wasn't as stupid as he seemed. If he started telling everyone that the Donkey couldn't work wonders, they might not accept its orders.

'Wonder Rub,' Muncle whispered, with what breath he had left.

Titan loosened the Chain a little. 'What?' he asked suspiciously.

'I'll get some ... Wonder ... Rub from the Wonder Donkey,' Muncle croaked, thinking on his feet. 'Then you can be a Guardsman again.'

Titan scowled. This clearly wasn't the answer he'd been expecting. 'You will?' he said.

'I will. But you have to promise me that if it works you'll never bully me again.'

Titan let go of the Chain. 'Done!' he said. 'Either your Wonder Rub heals my feet or I bully you for the rest of your life – AND tell everyone your donkey's a useless cheat.'

chapter fourteen

Muncle went home. Draggly looked up as he opened the door, and trotted across the room to nuzzle him.

'Hey, you're walking a lot better,' said Muncle. Very gently he unwrapped Draggly's bandages. Underneath, his feet were all the colours of the rainbow.

'Ma, could you put some Mustard Mend in a jar for me? I might need it.'

Ma sighed as she spooned ointment from her large jar into one small enough to fit into Muncle's old school-bag. 'I suppose people won't be wanting my medicines much longer,' she said. 'You'll be able to get them wonder cures from your Wonder Donkey.'

'Ma, we need your medicines as much as ever. I may never see the Wonder Donkey again. It's really important that people don't start thinking there'll be

wonders to solve all our problems. We've got to solve them ourselves. He sighed too. 'I've got to go out again, but I'll be back for supper.'

People were just starting to leave work for the day and Muncle guessed he'd find Titan with his friends in the cafe they'd always used to go to after school. He was right. It took Muncle a lot of courage to step inside.

'What are you doing here?' growled Titan. 'This is Thunder Thugs territory.'

'The whole town is Wise Man territory,' Muncle said bravely. 'I believe you wanted some of this.' He handed over the small jar.

'What's that?' said Thumper.

'Wonder Rub,' said Muncle.

'Wonder Rub?' said one of Titan's less close friends. 'Is there something wrong with you, Titan?'

'No!' snapped Titan. 'There's nothing wrong with me at all.'

Muncle fled home before things could turn nasty.

He'd hardly shut the door behind him when it burst open again.

'Git!' shouted Flubb as Gritt bounced into the room looking very pleased with himself. The door banged shut behind him and Pa emerged sleepily from his bed-in-the-wall, woken by the noise.

'Good day at school?' Ma asked Gritt.

'The best ever! Everyone's talking about Muncle and the Wonder Donkey. Everyone wants to be my friend. And they can't wait for dragon-riding lessons. When are we going to start, Muncle?'

'As soon as the dragons are mended. But there's a problem.' Muncle emptied the shopping bag on to the table.

'What are these silly little things?' asked Pa, picking up one of the pink stickies.

'They're not silly at all. They're what the Wonder Donkey gave me for mending dragon wings. But I haven't got nearly enough.'

Flubb picked up a sticky and tried to eat it. Ma took it from her and sniffed it.

'How do they work?' she said. 'Is it medicine or wonderness?'

'I'm not sure. I think they're just sticky.'

'You'll have to ask the Wonder Donkey for some more,' said Gritt.

Muncle knew he couldn't do that. Emily had used up all her money, and he was pretty sure that Smalling shops wouldn't take giant nuggets and nugglins.

'I can't just go and see the Wonder Donkey,' he said. Which was true – he knew where Emily lived, but he could hardly go and knock on her door.

Ma was still studying the little pink patch. 'But it's not sticky at all,' she said.

Muncle pulled off the backing and showed her the sticky stuff underneath. She licked it.

'*Bleeuugh*!'

'What's the matter, Ma? Is it nasty? *Poisonous*?'

'Itth thtuck to my tongue!'

'Oh!' Muncle giggled, and peeled the pink patch off her purple tongue with some difficulty.

'That's. *Really*. Sticky,' said Ma, scrubbing her tongue with a pine-cone toothbrush after each word. 'As sticky as a snail.'

Muncle stared at her and one of his best ideas exploded into his hurting head.

'Ma, you've got it! Pa, tonight you must hunt for nothing but snails and slugs. You and every other hunter. Bring them home alive. Tell them it's Wonder Donkey orders. And Ma, will you please collect spare bed sheets from every home, and tear them into strips three fingers wide? I'll get the Town Crier to announce that we need slugs and sheets and volunteers.'

'What?' said Gritt.

'Why?' said Pa.

'Is that three of your fingers or three of mine?' asked Ma.

'Three of yours. We're going to make our own stickies.'

For once, Muncle was lucky. That night it rained, and the slugs and snails were out in force. By the time the moon was up, the first sackfuls arrived in the Crater. And so did the volunteers, eager to help with what the Town Crier had announced as The Wonder Donkey's Operation Sticky.

Muncle looked around anxiously to see if Titan was there. It would be a disaster if he started telling the volunteers not to bother with Operation Sticky because the Wonder Donkey was a cheat. But there was no sign of Titan or any of his friends from the Thunder Thugs. They probably didn't want to lose a night's sleep.

Relieved, Muncle set everyone to work. The grown-ups tore the sheets into strips, and rolled them out along the Crater floor, and the children organised slug and snail races up and down them. Soon the strips were covered with trails of slime and were even stickier than Emily's pink patches.

They worked until dawn, and even then Muncle wouldn't let them eat any of the slugs or snails for breakfast.

'We must keep them in the sacks for a day or two until we're sure we've got enough stickies,' he said, as the first rays of sun spilt over the rim of the Crater and the Dragon Division appeared for their morning exercises.

Muncle cancelled the exercises and got them wing-mending instead. The long strips were much quicker to apply than Emily's little patches, and stronger too. Soon they were all patched up, and then the school dragons were brought out and mended too. By the time the dinner gong sounded, they were all flexing their wings with great interest. But just as people started taking their dragons back to their stables there was a low rumbling noise from somewhere near the Royal Palace. It grew steadily louder and louder – and ended in a thunderous crash and a cloud of smoke.

A Common Green school dragon burst through the cloud, coughing and flapping frantically as it skimmed clumsily over the heads of people in the Crater. And it wasn't alone. More dragons came, red and green, and then a handsome purple one, its wings clamped firmly to its sides as it galloped along with the Captain hanging on to its tail.

'What's happening?' Muncle cried as the Captain lost his grip and skidded to a halt beside him.

'Landslide,' he gasped. 'I'd just gone to the palace stables to mend the King's Rainbow Royals when the whole of the stable floor just slid down into the King's ale-warming cellar.'

'Oh no!' cried Muncle. 'What's happened to the Rainbow Royals?'

Before he could answer, more terrified dragons rushed past, knocking the Captain off his feet. A few had got the hang of flying straight away, but most hadn't. They bumped into each other. They crash-landed. They snorted and screeched. Muncle felt as though he was in the middle of a storm with dragons as hailstones. And in the middle of it all, school children and Guardsmen were trying to run to safety.

Think of the chaos, Biblos had said. He'd been right.

Muncle would never get everyone to Back of Beyond at this rate.

'Move aside, minikin!' shouted a shrill voice behind him.

Muncle jumped out of the way just in time as the largest dragon he had ever seen came charging out of the dust cloud.

It was Reks, the King's finest and most famous Rainbow Royal. On its back sat a small, determined-looking figure, blowing furiously on a jewelled dragon flute.

Puglug.

'The Crown Princess!' gasped the Captain, covering his eyes with both hands. 'She'll never control such a big dragon. She's going to fall off!'

But the Princess didn't *fall* off – she *took* off. As Reks's rainbow wings passed over his head Muncle could clearly see dozens of pink stickies.

'Blistering bogspots!' cried Muncle. 'She's mended Reks herself!'

'Look at me!' yelled Puglug, waving as King Thortless's finest Rainbow Royal soared higher and higher. 'Look at me! I'm flying!'

Chapter fifteen

Muncle blew the loudest 'Come Here' of his life.

Within seconds Snarg was circling above the Crater, puffing out little flames of welcome.

'Here, boy,' Muncle shouted, and he blew his 'Land' signal.

Snarg circled twice more. But he could see for himself that there was no longer anything to be afraid of – all Mount Grumble's dragons were flying now. He swooped down, clearing himself a path between the clumsy learners, and landed on the Crater floor.

Muncle scrambled on board and took off, climbing through the smoke and dust. He had to persuade the Princess to come home.

Reks was circling higher and higher on the warm smoky air. Shafts of sunlight broke through the clouds and glinted off his multicoloured scales. He looked almost as magnificent as Puglug, who was wearing a black-and-white outfit of badger-skin riding breeches and magpie-feather cloak.

'You look splendid, Your Hugeness ...' called Muncle.

'I do, don't I?' said Puglug.

'... but you shouldn't be flying up here.'

'But the Wonder Donkey wants us to!'

'Not out of the Crater. You might get lost in the cloud.'

He had to get her safely home. If Puglug fell off, Muncle would get the blame. He'd lose his job and with it the only chance of getting everyone to Back of Beyond.

'You see all this smoke, Your Hugeness?' he said quickly. 'Why do you think there's so much of it?'

'How should I know?' said the Princess. 'You haven't taught me anything about smoke.'

'It's because everyone's got their cooking fires going. Didn't you hear the dinner-gong?'

'*Dinner-time*?' Puglug's eyes widened again.

She didn't know Muncle's new signal for

'Land' but she quickly blew 'Sit Down' and 'Lie Down', and Reks plunged into the Crater.

'Too steep!' gasped Muncle, as Snarg dived after the Princess.

But Puglug hung on and Reks seemed to know how to save himself. At the last moment he raised his head and landed in the Crater on his belly with a loud SMACK, sliding to a stop right outside the palace doors.

As Puglug slid from Reks's back a Guardsman ran to catch her, but Queen Fattipat got there first. She slung the Princess over her shoulder and carried her, wailing, into the palace. Puglug had obviously not had her ma's permission to go flying.

Oh dear, poor Puglug, Muncle thought as Snarg landed. *But if only everyone could learn to fly that well, maybe I'd have a chance of getting everyone to Back of Beyond after all.*

Muncle was in the Crater early the next morning. He guessed that Puglug would try to go flying again and he couldn't risk that. Besides, he had a job for her. He sat down to wait outside the palace stables with Piglitt in his lap. There was no one else there. The Crater was deserted. Everyone was exhausted after the previous day of wing-mending and dragon chaos.

Before long the stable doors opened. The landslide had left a mess of rubble and dust, and it wasn't easy to get in and out. Puglug scrambled out first, heaving on Reks's chain, and the dragon squeezed out after her.

The Princess climbed quickly up the dragon's tail and along his spiny backbone as if it was a ladder.

What a brilliant way of getting on board, thought Muncle. *I wish I'd thought of that.*

Puglug settled herself on a sheepskin cushion and put her flute to her lips. But before she could blow it, Muncle stepped out quickly from behind the stable door.

'I'm not having a lesson this morning,' snapped Puglug. She climbed down, snatched Piglitt and tucked her up in a doll's cradle strapped to Reks's back.

'No, you're not,' agreed Muncle. 'You're *giving* a lesson.'

Puglug's black eyes opened wide. 'You want *me* to teach *you*?'

'Not me,' he said. 'But you did really well on your first flight yesterday, Your Hugeness, so I want you and Reks to teach the school children to fly, while Snarg and I teach the army.'

'Oopdeedoopdee!' cried Puglug. 'When do we start?'

'Right now!'

Once Muncle had whistled for Snarg – and climbed onboard using Puglug's up-the-tail method – he rode quickly to the school and the King's Guard Barracks. As soon as the gong went, the whole school lined up on one side of the Crater for a special Dragon Studies lesson. The Dragon Division lined up for flying exercises on the other side.

The dragons were all flexing and flapping their newly-mended wings. Some of them flapped so strongly that they almost took off before their riders had had time to climb on board. Muncle didn't want anyone flying till he'd shown them how to do it properly.

'You stay here, please, Your Hugeness, and make sure no-one takes off yet,' he said. 'I want to show them what the new signals are before they have a go themselves.'

He blew 'Up Up Up' and Snarg took off. They showed everyone the signals for 'Turn Right' and 'Turn

Left' and 'Land'. Snarg did it all perfectly, using his wings as brakes and landing neatly, back feet first.

Reks was desperate to take off. It took three soldiers to hang on to his chain. Puglug bounced up and down on his back. 'Let him go, guards!' she cried. 'Let him go!'

'No!' shouted Muncle. 'He's got to learn that he can only fly when he's told to. Blow the signal first, Your Hugeness, and *then* they can let go.'

Puglug blew 'Up Up Up'.

The soldiers let go.

Reks took off.

'Turn Right!' shouted Muncle. 'Left! Now Land!'

'But I don't want to land,' Puglug shouted back. 'I want to go exploring.'

'No!' Muncle's little shout was drowned out by a louder one. 'Come back at once, Puglug,' shouted King Thortless, waving frantically from the royal balcony.

'Don't want to.' Puglug yelled, giving her pa a cheeky wave as she flew past the balcony.

'Flying is not for royalty,' the King cried.

'Flying is for everyone in Mount Grumble,' Puglug yelled back. 'Wonder Donkey's orders.'

'Even *me*?' said the King, faintly.

'Even you, Pa,' Puglug said. 'You can be my passenger. Why don't you have a go now?'

'No time,' said the King. 'I have matters of State to attend to.' He shot back into the palace and the balcony door slammed behind him.

At last Reks got tired and Puglug landed.

'You do understand about not flying out of the Crater, Your Hugeness, don't you?' Muncle said, anxiously. 'Remember The Law with Respect to Smallings – "Keep in the cloud, keep to the night, keep in the mine, keep out of sight ..."'

'All right, all right,' said Puglug sulkily, 'but flying's soon going to get boring if we can only go round and round the Crater.'

She was right. Before long he would have to think of a way of making flying more exciting. But while everyone was still learning it should be exciting enough.

'You take the children, Your Hugeness, and get them to copy you, one at a time, until their dragons have all learnt to take off and land when they hear the signals. I'll do the same with the soldiers.'

Soon there was lots of coming and going on Puglug's side of the Crater, as one dragon took off and another landed. There were far more children than school dragons, so some rode two to a dragon and took turns to drive.

On Muncle's side of the Crater things were not going quite so well. The army dragons were keen enough, and so were most of the soldiers. Except for one. The Captain wasn't keen at all. He clung on to Pompom's neck for dear life.

'Take off!' Muncle yelled at him for the third time.

'I can't. Er ... my dragon flute still isn't working.'

Muncle could plainly hear the Captain's flute, and judging by the way his ears were swivelling, so could Pompom. But he had sensed his rider's fear and was trembling himself. Muncle had to find some way of coaxing him into the air.

'Let me have a go, Captain,' he said.

The Captain was only too happy to get off. Muncle ran up Pompom's tail, sat down and pulled firmly on the dragon's collar as he blew 'Up Up Up'. Pompom took off at once. He wobbled a bit but soon fell into a steady wing-flapping rhythm. Muncle flew him twice round the Crater and then landed, pulling on his collar at the last minute to bring up his head and make sure he landed back feet first. He jumped off and handed Pompom back to the Captain.

'Now you do it,' he said.

The Captain was still shaking with fear, but Pompom was enjoying himself now. He swooped and looped round the Crater and when he landed the Captain fell off, looking green. But at least he'd done it. All that morning's learners could now fly if they had to.

The Town Crier banged the gong for dinner-time. Puglug dashed off to the palace, but Muncle just bought himself a mole-in-a-roll from a market stall and carried on teaching, because everyone else had begun to lead their guard-dragons into the Crater to join in the flying lessons.

The taking-off and landing began all over again and a large crowd collected as people waited for their turn. They stamped and cheered as they watched their friends and neighbours sailing into the air and bumping back down to earth. It was noisier than the King's Birthday and the Victory Feast put together. Every giant was there, and all afternoon the Crater shook with the stamping and bumping.

Everything was going really well. But then, just as the King's Guard were going into their Barracks for supper, the whole building fell down with an almighty crash.

Chapter sixteen

'What happened? What *happened*?' Muncle shouted, to no-one in particular.

There was a gaping hole in the Crater wall and clouds of dust rose from a huge pile of rubble where moments ago the Barracks had stood. Screaming giants and screeching dragons rushed to the other side of the Crater as fast as they could.

'I'll tell you what happened.' The Captain crawled out of the rubble, struggling to remove his head from his dented helmet. 'All these dragons flapping their wings made such a wind that it blew my Barracks down.'

'It wasn't the dragons,' Muncle said desperately. He couldn't have the Captain telling people that flying lessons were the problem. This was the most serious volcano warning yet, and flying was the only thing that could save them if the whole town fell down.

Help came from somewhere rather unexpected.

The floor of the army Barracks was also the roof of the dungeons. And ragged, sooty prisoners were scrambling up through the rubble, handcuffed to ragged, sooty prison guards.

The ragged, sooty Dungeon Master limped from the ruined building. 'It was the Central Heating,' he said. 'Goo suddenly burst up through every cell in the dungeons and set fire to the tree trunks that hold up the roof.'

'Fire!' cried the Captain. 'Fire! Send for the Fire Brigade!'

The Goo had brought down a building! Muncle felt his heart drop into his belly.

He thought quickly. Other buildings would fall down very soon indeed if the fire spread. It had to be put out. Flames were beginning to appear underneath the rubble. The firemen wouldn't be able to get to them with their fire-beating brooms. He remembered what Emily had told him about the Smalling Fire Brigade. 'What we need is water,' he said to the Captain.

'Of course you don't want *water*, wibblewit!' shouted the Captain, quite forgetting to treat the King's Wise Man with the Utmost Respect. He ran off yelling for the Fire Brigade.

The Crater was still crowded with giants and dragons who weren't sure whether it was safer to stay outdoors or go home.

'Gritt!' Muncle shouted, spotting his brother astride a school dragon. 'Quick! Round up your friends and go to all the shops, grubhouses and alehouses. Borrow as many buckets as you can. Fill them at the Crater pump and carry them to the fire. Pour the water down the gaps in the rubble and keep going till the fire's out.'

'Yes, sir, Muncle!' cried Gritt, saluting like a Guardsman, and he turned to his class. 'You heard the Wise Man! Water!'

Muncle flew Snarg low over the rubble. Before long he could see Gritt's dragon galloping across the Crater, followed by a crowd of school dragons and classmates. Gritt had one hand on his dragon's collar and a bucket of water in the other. His best friend Tuff sat behind him, carefully balanced with a bucket in each hand. Clouds of steam rose from their buckets. Fart-flavoured steam.

Steam? Surely you needed *cold* water to put out hot fire?

'No, Gritt,' Muncle called to him. 'I meant you to get the buckets from the grubhouses, but the water from the pump.'

'We *did*.' Gritt emptied his bucket on to the rubble. 'It was steaming when it came out of the pump.'

'*What*?'

Tuff emptied his buckets, and some of the flames went out with a hiss and a puff of black smoke, but that didn't do much to cheer Muncle up. The water shouldn't be hot – or fart-flavoured. Hadn't Emily said something about fart smells being another warning sign?

Gritt and his friends did a good job. By the time the Captain came back with the Fire Brigade, the flames were out. But the collapse of the Barracks had put an end to flying practice, and as the firemen flapped feebly at the smoke with their brooms the supper-time gong rang out. There was no chance of getting the practice started again now.

The most flying anyone had managed was a few laps of the Crater. To get to Back of Beyond they would have to fly for days.

They needed to practise for longer flights. They needed to practise finding their way through cloud. Was there enough time?

Once the last flame was out Muncle flew Snarg to the museum. The crash of the falling building had been so loud that Biblos would have heard it even without his ear-trumpet. He would be worried.

But so were a lot of other people. As Muncle tied Snarg to an iron ring at the foot of the museum steps, a group of frightened giants gathered round him. Frightened – and angry.

'That's right, minikin,' snarled a blacksmith with arms as thick and gnarled as the trunk of an ancient oak. 'You go and give that Chain back to Biblos. We want our proper Wise Man back. We never had trouble like this when he was in charge.'

Snarg shot a blast of fiery breath at him, but it landed harmlessly on his thick leather apron.

Muncle started to back up the museum steps but a worried woman seized him by the jerkin.

'What's going on?' she asked anxiously. 'Why did the army building fall down? Is the Wonder Donkey angry with us?'

'No, of course not,' said Muncle, trying to stop his

voice wobbling. 'The Wonder Donkey is very pleased with the way we've all started to fly. Just keep practising, everybody, and the Wonder Donkey will look after us.'

'But one young man has been telling me the Wonder Donkey can't work wonders at all,' cried an even more anxious woman. 'He says if it could, it would have made you giant-sized by now.'

Muncle didn't need to ask which young man she meant. Titan.

'The Wonder Donkey wanted to,' he said, dashing up the steps before anyone could see that he was close to tears. 'But I wouldn't let it. I *like* being this size.'

He found Biblos waiting for him in the museum doorway, his face as white as his beard.

'There's so much noise I can't work out what's going on,' he said, shaking his ear trumpet. 'Has there been another landslide?'

'Sort of,' said Muncle. He didn't want to alarm Biblos with reports of Goo starting fires and bringing down buildings before he'd thought of a way of getting the old man to fly.

'Muncle, your Wonder Donkey should be making life better for us, but it seems to be making things worse. We never had landslides like this before it came. Are you sure it's a *real* Wonder Donkey?'

Muncle was glad that the sun had dropped below the top of Mount Grumble, throwing the Crater into deep shade. Biblos wouldn't notice that he'd suddenly turned pale.

'What do you mean, *real*?' he said shakily.

'I mean can you be sure it's not a Smalling trick? Something to do with the girl who escaped?'

'Emily?' squeaked Muncle. How had Biblos found out?

'Yes. What if she got home safely and told her people all about us? What if your donkey wasn't a Wonder Donkey from Back of Beyond at all, but an Evil Donkey, full of Smalling spells and sent to destroy us?'

As Biblos shuffled back into the museum, Reks glided past, silent as an owl. He was flying just as well as Snarg now.

'Everyone else is going home,' Puglug called. 'They're fed up with flying. But I'm going flying properly. Out of the Crater.'

'No!' said Muncle. 'No, you mustn't. The Law with Respect to Smallings, remember!'

'I *have* remembered – "Keep in the cloud, keep to the night". Well, it's cloudy now, and it'll soon be night. Let's have a race – to the moon and back!'

Muncle looked at the moon hanging low between the clouds over the rim of Mount Grumble. A race would be good practice for the long journey. Which was nearer – the moon or Back of Beyond?

'Excellent plan, Your Hugeness! We could have lots of races, and get everyone else to join in too.'

Puglug's black eyes gleamed. 'Ooh, yes! Let's call it Fly-By-Night, and have competitions too, just like Warts 'n' All, with prizes for the Most Dashing Dragon and Finest Fashionable Flyer.'

Muncle grinned. He could guess who would win those titles. 'We may not have time to organise all that,' he said, 'but we'll make it as much fun as we can. You go and tell your ma and pa to get ready to present the prizes, and I'll tell the Town Crier to announce it to the whole town right away. Everyone will just have time to get their supper before it gets properly dark and we can start the races.'

'Oopdeedoopdee!' cried Puglug. 'Races! Prizes!'

Chapter seventeen

Muncle ate a quick supper of otter 'otpot.

'Are you sure this is a good idea?' Ma asked him.

'It's a brilliant idea,' said Gritt. 'Fly-by-Night here I come!'

'No, I didn't mean the races and competitions. I meant having them *tonight*. Wouldn't it be better to give yourself a few days to organise them properly?'

'Maybe we haven't *got* a few days,' said Pa. 'Maybe tomorrow the whole town's going to fall down, just like the Barracks.'

'*What*?' said Ma faintly.

'I'm just repeating what everyone else is saying,' said Pa.

'Everyone?' Muncle's heart sank. He'd hoped it had just been a few people.

'What *are* they saying?' said Gritt.

'I'm sorry, but you need to know. Some people are saying the Wonder Donkey has deserted us. And others are saying buildings never fell down when Biblos was Wise Man.'

'That's not fair!' said Gritt. 'Biblos never had a visit from the Wonder Donkey. Muncle's a much better Wise Man than Biblos.'

'Of course he is.' Ma sat down beside Muncle and put her huge arm round his skinny shoulders. 'You should have stuck up for him, Pa.'

'I tried.' Pa was looking very uncomfortable. 'The trouble is, a lot of people seem to think Muncle himself is the problem.'

'*Me*?'

'It's because you're Smalling size. People are saying that the Smallings are sending their magic through you into Mount Grumble.'

Ma gasped. 'You mean they've put a curse on him?' She held him away from her and looked deep into his eyes.

Muncle took a deep breath. 'Of course they haven't put a curse on me, Ma. And the Wonder Donkey hasn't deserted us. That's not the trouble. The trouble is

Mount Grumble itself. The trouble is Goo. I haven't told everyone yet because I didn't want to worry people until they'd learnt to fly. But they can fly now. I'll tell them tonight, after the races.'

'Muncle what *are* you talking about?' Ma often looked anxious, but not as anxious as she was looking now.

'It's all right, Ma, there's nothing to worry about. Come on, it's time to go. Pa and Gritt, will you come to the museum with me? Biblos must come to Fly-by-Night and he can't walk far. I want you to bring him in his carry-chair.'

'How long is this Fly-by-Night going to take?' said Ma, as she hoisted Flubb's baby-basket on to her back. 'I don't like to leave Draggly on his own for too long.'

'Draggly had better come too,' said Muncle.

The Crater was already milling with giants and dragons. Torches had been lit and grubhouses and market stalls that had closed for the day were hurriedly being opened again in the hope of some unexpected trade. But no-one seemed to see Fly-by-Night as a fun night out. They were grumbling as loudly as the mountain.

'Thrumbles,' said Ma. 'It's hotter than ever.'

'It's because we're all crowded together,' said Muncle. 'It'll be cooler when everyone spreads out on the mountain top to watch the races. Just follow the Town Crier's instructions, Ma, and find us a good place to watch . We'll join you as soon as we've collected Biblos.'

'Fly-by-Night!' boomed the Town Crier. 'Giants and giantesses, make your way to the top of Mount Grumble! Plenty of room for all your dragons on the top of Mount Grumble! Fly-by-Night!'

But no-one seem very keen to go. As he pushed his way through the crowd to the museum Muncle overheard little bits of conversation.

'Stupid plan. My dragon's tired out. We don't want to go racing.'

'*Wise* Man? *Wibblewit* Man if you ask me.'

'If this is the Wonder Donkey's idea, where is it? That's what I'd like to know.'

'If that Wonder Donkey really wanted to help us it wouldn't have disappeared when Mount Grumble started falling down.'

Muncle looked up and saw Ma scrambling up the steep path to the summit with Flubb asleep on her back and Draggly on a lead. Very few people seemed to be following her. What had seemed like a good idea to him and Puglug clearly didn't seem so to everyone else.

People needed to see that Biblos was going. Maybe then they would change their minds.

Pa and Gritt followed Muncle to the museum. The door was ajar. Muncle pushed it open. A single candle flickered inside, lighting up a heap of straggly hair and string-cloth clothes.

Biblos was lying flat on his face on the floor.

'Biblos!' cried Muncle, dropping to his knees beside him. Nervously he reached out a hand. Was he dead?

Biblos groaned. He wasn't dead – but he didn't sound at all well.

'Gritt,' said Muncle, 'run and find Ma. We need medicine.'

But before Gritt could go anywhere, Muncle spotted a pink sparkly bag on the floor next to Biblos. A soft 'Ee-Aw!' came from the shadows.

Muncle spun round. 'Em...!' he cried, before turning the word quickly into a cough.

'The Wonder Donkey!' gasped Pa and Gritt. They threw themselves to the floor, and Muncle hurriedly bowed down himself.

'EE-AW.' Emily shuffled out of the shadows.

Muncle quickly straightened up again. 'What are you doing here?' he whispered.

'I had to come,' she whispered back. 'We've been given a Red Alert.'

Muncle looked into Emily's eyes through the holes in the donkey's neck. They were round with fear. She was serious. Mount Grumble was about to erupt. There was no time to lose. 'Say Ee-Aw,' he whispered.

'EE-AW, EE-AW,' Emily said out loud.

'Get up, everyone,' Muncle said. He picked up Biblos's ear-trumpet and held it to the old man's ear. 'The Wonder Donkey wants you all to go to Fly-by-Night right away.'

Pa helped Biblos to his feet and they both stared in awe at the Wonder Donkey. Gritt was still on his knees, his mouth gaping wide.

'Fly-by-Night?' said the old man. 'What is this Fly-by-Night? The Town Crier has been shouting about it all evening. Is it something to do with the Wonder Donkey?'

'No,' said Muncle, and then, as he had another idea, 'I mean yes. Wonder Donkey's orders. Pa, will you and Gritt take Biblos up the mountain?'

'What's going on?' protested the old man as Pa lifted him into his carry-chair. 'Why am I going up the mountain?'

'I'll explain on the way,' said Pa. 'Hold on to your ear-trumpet, Biblos, you're going to need it.' He took the front handles and Gritt took the back, and they carried the old man out into the night.

'Phew,' said Emily as soon as they'd gone. She wriggled her arms free, pushed off the donkey head and collapsed on to a footstool. 'I've been here for hours. When it started to get dark I was afraid you wouldn't come till morning.'

'Is it really a Red Alert?'

Emily nodded. 'I wouldn't have come otherwise,' she said. 'It was hard to get away – I told Mum I was going round to a friend's to get back some books I'd lent her. Everyone's packing and trying to decide what to take and what to leave behind. It's going mad at home. I have to get back as soon as I can.'

'It's going mad here too, what with dragons learning to fly and the Barracks falling down.'

'Buildings falling down? Oh no! That must have been the big shock the scientists picked up on their instruments. That's when the alert changed to Red. Muncle, I was lucky to even get here. There are cracks in the forest floor and the stream seems to have changed course. It was hard to find the way. You must leave at once. There's no time to lose.'

'I know,' said Muncle, desperately. 'But first we have to get everyone flying. We haven't had nearly enough practice to get every giant and dragon all the way to Back of Beyond. That's why we're having Fly-By-Night.'

'What's that?'

'Races. It was Puglug's idea, really. We had to think of something to make flying practice fun. We're racing to the moon and back.'

'You're *what*?' Emily spluttered.

'Racing. To the moon and back. What's the matter? Is there something wrong with that?'

'Muncle, do you know how far away the moon is? It would take for ever to fly there on a dragon. And you'd die before you got there, because there isn't any air to breathe once you get a long way from the earth.'

'Oh.' Muncle believed her. She'd been right about volcanoes so she was probably right about the moon too. Smallings seemed to know so much.

'You can still have races, though,' said Emily. 'Why don't you just fly round and round the mountain top?'

'Well, I suppose we could do that,' said Muncle.

'Of course you could. But will you please give me a lift home first? I'm afraid of getting lost now the forest has changed – and Mum and Dad must be worried about me by now.'

Muncle hesitated. Emily had done so much for Mount Grumble already, but he had to ask her one last favour. 'Emily, since the Barracks fell down people are saying the Wonder Donkey has deserted us. They think it's because I'm a bad Wise Man. But if you come, everyone will see that you *haven't* deserted us and they'll trust me again.'

'Muncle, I—'

'*Please*, Emily. I need you more than ever. Biblos and Pa and Gritt have already seen you – they'll be really worried if you desert us again. And everyone will be so excited if you hand out the prizes.'

Emily looked torn, then she sighed. 'I can't stay long, Muncle …'

Muncle gave her a very gentle 'thank you' hug. She really was the best friend he'd ever had. The only one, really.

Emily put on her donkey head and squeezed her arms back into the suit.

'Can you bring my bag?' she said. 'It keeps falling off my shoulder when my arms are inside this suit.'

Muncle slung Emily's pink sparkly bag over his own shoulder. Together they hurried out on to the museum steps and Muncle blew his flute. A few giants and dragons were up on the mountain top now, but far more were still in the Crater, complaining about having to do more flying when it was nearly bed-time. It was only the heat and smoke in the Crater that was making them climb further up the mountain where the air was cleaner and cooler.

Snarg swooped down and Muncle helped Emily on board. This was his last chance to save the giants. If they wouldn't come to the Fly-By-Night practice they'd all go up in flames with Mount Grumble.

And it could happen at any moment.

Muncle's best Wise
Minikin face.

Chapter eighteen

Gasps went up from the crowd, followed by delighted cheers, when Muncle, Emily and Snarg soared above the Crater.

'It's the Wonder Donkey!'

'It hasn't deserted us!'

'Hooray for the Wonder Donkey!'

'Hooray for the Wise Minikin!'

Dragons and giants bowed down.

'Oh, not all that again,' said Emily. 'EE-AW, EE-AW.'

'The Wonder Donkey wants every giant and dragon on top of the mountain,' shouted Muncle and the crowd started to stream up the steep paths.

Before long every giant and every dragon in Mount Grumble was on the mountain top – dragons that were too young to fly had been brought to watch, and those that were too young even to walk were being carried.

Emily gasped. 'So many dragons,' she whispered. 'There are hundreds of them. I never realised you had so many.'

While everyone settled down, Muncle circled the summit looking for somewhere to land. He spotted his family but they were in the middle of the crowd and he didn't dare join them – he didn't want anyone to look at the Wonder Donkey too closely. He found a rock sticking out some distance from everyone else. Snarg lay down on it, and Muncle and Emily stayed sitting comfortably on his back. From a ledge below, the Town Crier watched them land and then banged his gong.

BOIOIOING!

'We are honoured by the presence of the Wonder Donkey,' he boomed.

Muncle nudged Emily.

'EE-AW! EE-AW!'

'The Wonder Donkey says let Fly-by-Night begin!' shouted Muncle.

'Let Fly-by-Night begin!' yelled the Town Crier twenty times louder, and he banged his gong three times.

For a few moments nothing happened. Muncle looked expectantly at the Town Crier and noticed that he was looking expectantly into the Crater.

'What's going on?' said Emily, anxiously.

'I think those three boings must have been a signal for something.'

Sure enough, as they watched, a strange monster lumbered on to the palace balcony, lifted into the air and headed towards them.

It was Reks. The Princess sat in her usual driving position, with the little pig in her cradle behind her. But behind Piglitt were two thrones strapped to the dragon's back. And strapped to the thrones were King Thortless and Queen Fattipat, looking an interesting shade of green.

Puglug flew a lap of the mountain top, slowed down when she saw Muncle, and nearly fell off when she spotted Emily.

'It's the Wonder Donkey!' she exclaimed. 'What do you think of my Throne Dragon, Donkey?'

'EE-*AW*!' Emily shouted back.

The King's Groom had already taken the King's other Rainbow Royals up the mountain and had kept a space for Reks to land. It was quite near the Trogg family and Pa scrambled aside to make more room. The King and Queen seemed very glad to get off and sit on solid ground. But Puglug moved Piglitt to the second-best Rainbow Royal and got on to it herself. She obviously didn't want the weight of the thrones to spoil her chance in the races.

'Announce the first race,' she shouted to the Town Crier. 'To the moon! Last one back's a wibblewit!'

'No!' gasped Emily. 'EE-AW! *EE-AW*!'

'The Wonder Donkey says one lap of the mountain only,' Muncle yelled. 'And not everyone at once!'

BOIOIOING!

'First race,' shouted the Town Crier. 'Under-sevens. One lap of Mount Grumble.'

They lined up opposite Snarg's rock, Puglug on the second-best Rainbow Royal among them.

'We agreed the moon,' she shouted. 'I want to go to the moon.'

'The Wonder Donkey tells me that would take too long,' Muncle shouted back. 'We'll have to leave the moon for another night.'

The Town Crier hit his gong, leaving the Princess no time to argue. The under-sevens flew anti-sunwise round the top of Mount Grumble.

Puglug won. Of course.

She flew towards Muncle and the Wonder Donkey, grinning like a frog.

'Where are the prizes?' whispered Emily.

'Oh, blistering bogspots!' Muncle muttered. 'I haven't got any!'

'Quick, get the tube of sweets out of my bag.'

Muncle rummaged in the pink sparkly bag.

'No, not *that* – that's my torch. I'd never have found my way through the forest and your street-tunnels without it. There's another tube – a multi-coloured one. Hurry.'

Puglug, hovering on Reks, was getting impatient. 'I want my prize!' she said.

'Oink,' agreed Piglitt.

Muncle had no idea what multi-coloured meant, but he found another tube.

'Yes, that. Take off the little plastic lid at the end.'

He looked inside and frowned. 'Tablets?'

'They're sweets.'

They were tiny and all sorts of different colours. They didn't look much like the Lizard Licks and Earthworm Chews Muncle thought of as sweets. But they were all they had. Muncle put one on the palm of his hand and held it out to Puglug.

'EE-AW EE-AW!' said Emily.

'Congratulations from the Wonder Donkey,' said Muncle.

Puglug peered at the tiny sweet. 'What is it?' she said suspiciously.

'A wondersuck,' whispered Emily. 'EE-AW!'

'It's a wondersuck,' said Muncle, thinking quickly, 'to work wonders in your mouth.'

'Oh!' Puglug opened her enormous mouth and popped in the sweet. Her eyes opened wider and wider. 'Oooh,' she gasped. 'That's *wonder*ful! Can I go in for another race?'

'Not until everyone else has had their turn,' said Muncle. Puglug could already fly well – it was everyone else who needed to practise. He was afraid Puglug would throw one of her tantrums, but she just smiled, nodded and flew back to her parents.

Muncle was amazed. 'Emily, those sweets really *do* work wonders!'

'Not really,' Emily said. 'But the taste is amazing if you hadn't tried chocolate before. The orange ones are the best.'

Chocolate? What the thrumbles was that? Muncle tried one. It was sweet and crunchy on the outside, but the inside melted on his tongue and sent a thrilling glow right through him.

'Muncle, what's happening?' Emily suddenly clutched his arm. 'Why is the ground shaking?'

BOIOIOING!

'Er ... don't worry, Emily, the echo of the gong always makes the Crater tremble,' said Muncle, putting an arm around her shoulders. But everyone else had started looking anxious too. They knew this was more than the usual tremble, and so did he. He just needed to keep Emily calm till they finished the races.

'Next race, new army recruits, two laps!'

Emily huddled down, her long donkey nose resting on Snarg's back, as the soldiers flew past.

'Muncle, I want to go home. It's getting too dangerous.'

'Not long now, Emily. Just a few more races. *Please*?'

Emily sat up. Muncle heard a sharp intake of breath from inside the donkey head. 'Muncle, it's that thug who gave me to the King.'

She was right. In their uniforms and the dark, all the riders had looked much the same. But the winner now flying up for his prize really was Titan. And he was wearing his army boots. He was back in the King's Guard.

'I see your feet are better,' Muncle said casually as he gave Titan his prize.

Titan glared at him. Then he glared at the prize. 'What d'you call this?' he snarled, hurling the tiny sweet to the ground. 'Where's my gold medal, you cheating ...?'

Titan was interrupted by a long low rumble. It was followed by a huge shower of orange sparks from the Crater.

'No medals tonight,' said Muncle shakily. 'Fireworks instead.'

But half the crowd were already screaming at the 'fireworks' – and not with delight. The Wonder Donkey on Snarg's back shook like frogspawn jelly. Its head tilted dangerously.

'Help!' squeaked Emily faintly. 'I want my mum!'

'That donkey of yours isn't a Wonder,' said Titan. 'It probably isn't even a donkey. There's something wrong with its head.'

Muncle took a deep breath. 'The Wonder Donkey's special powers let it move any way it wants,' he said. 'It can turn its head all the way round like an owl.'

'Special powers?' snorted Titan. 'It's no more special than I am.'

At the same moment a series of notes rang out shrilly close by. It was like no dragon flute Muncle had ever heard before and the few dragons within earshot backed away hurriedly as if the noise hurt.

Snarg snorted and swung his head round sharply. And Titan's dragon reared up and threw him into the Crater.

Emily sat up and started to wriggle frantically inside her suit. 'Phone,' she whispered frantically. 'In my bag.'

Phone? Another word he didn't know. Muncle opened the pink sparkly bag again. A tiny flat box inside was glowing and shivering. Whatever Emily might say, it had to be Smalling magic. The donkey head wobbled violently and tilted to one side. A small pink hand shot out of the donkey suit and grabbed the box. Muncle just had time to see Emily clamp it to her ear before the donkey head fell back into place and the box stopped ringing.

'I'm sorry, Mum,' Muncle heard her say. 'I didn't mean to stay out so late. We just got talking and I didn't ... *what*?'

There was a lot of high-pitched squeaking inside the donkey head.

'All right, Mum,' Emily said tearfully, 'all right, I'm coming straight away.' She turned to Muncle. 'Please take me home, quick. Everybody's been ordered out of town. My parents are leaving in one hour!'

Down below them the crowd hadn't heard the ringing noise above Mount Grumble's rumbles, and the Town Crier was starting another race. But Muncle couldn't ask Emily to stay any longer. He should never have made her come in the first place.

BOIOIOING!

The ground shook even more violently.

CRASH!

A huge cloud of smoke and ash rose in an almighty explosion from the Crater below, followed by a fountain of rock and Goo. The Royal Palace was hurled into the air in a thousand pieces.

Emily screamed.

Snarg jumped clear as the rock he was lying on began to crumble. Muncle clung on, but Emily, her arms trapped inside the donkey suit, slipped sideways.

Muncle tried to grab her, but it was too late. She slipped out of his grasping hands, and on to the Crater rim, just as Snarg spread his wings and glided clear of the mountain.

'Land!' Muncle blew frantically. 'Land! Lie Down! Sit down!'

Snarg took no notice. Mount Grumble was roaring, giants were roaring, dragons were roaring. Muncle wasn't sure that Snarg could even hear his dragon flute above the din.

Helplessly he watched as Emily fought her way out of the donkey suit. He looked round anxiously, but he was the only one who'd seen the Wonder Donkey fall. Everyone else was staring into the Crater in horror and disbelief. It was bubbling like a huge cauldron of orange porridge.

Emily didn't look round at all. As soon as she was out of the suit she started scrambling down the mountainside as fast as she could. Within moments she was out of sight.

Chapter nineteen

Muncle and Snarg flew low over the mountainside and forest, searching for Emily, but it was no use. The air was thick with smoke and dust, and Muncle could hardly see beyond Snarg's nose. The Smalling town wasn't far – Emily was probably there already. There was nothing he could do to help her now, and there were a lot of giants on the mountain who needed him too. The Wise Man had to help everyone.

He turned back to the mountain top, and flew blindly through the ash cloud, coughing and blowing the 'Take Off' signal over and over again. But he couldn't see anyone. Where were they? Muncle started to feel desperate. Had they heard the signal? Had they practised it enough to remember it? Then, through a break in the ash cloud, came a wonderful sight.

Dragons. Hundreds and hundreds of them. Common Greens, Common Reds, Purple Nobles and the few precious Rainbow Royals. And they were all flying – soaring – into the air, just as if they were born to fly. Which, of course, they were.

It was all Muncle could do not to cry with relief.

Puglug flew past on the second-best Rainbow Royal with the King and Queen clinging to its spines and a startled-looking Piglitt peeping out of the cradle.

'Fly north!' Muncle yelled. 'To Back of Beyond!'

'Oopdedoopdee!' Puglug yelled back. 'I've always wanted to go to Back of Beyond. We'll have Dwelfs for servants and there'll be enough Wonder Donkeys for us to have one each.'

'Slow down!' yelled the King. 'My crown's just blown off.'

'Mine too,' cried Puglug, 'but who cares? Follow me, everyone! Last one there's a wibblewit!'

Just behind her, Reks loomed out of the cloud – with Gritt driving and Ma and Pa strapped safely into the thrones behind. Ma had Draggly and Flubb clasped tight in her arms. Muncle sighed with relief again, and this time a tear escaped down his cheek.

'I didn't steal him, Muncle,' shouted Gritt. 'Honest!'

'I know,' yelled Muncle, grinning broadly. 'Well done!'

'Come with us, Muncle!' cried Ma.

'Don't worry. I'll catch you up. Fly! Fly north to Back of Beyond. Drive safely, Gritt.'

'That's right,' yelled Pa from the King's throne. 'No upside-downing!'

Within moments they were out of earshot, but dragon after dragon kept coming. Pompom flew confidently past – the Captain had tied himself on with rope, while his wife did the driving. Another Purple Noble came puffing by with a heavy load – the Town Crier had brought his gong with him, as well as his wife and ten children. And then dragons came so thick and fast that Muncle didn't have time to recognise everyone.

'Come on, Snarg,' said Muncle at last, when he thought the last dragon had flown past. 'We must check that no-one's been left behind.'

Slowly they circled the mountain top. Halfway round Muncle spotted a lone figure, still in his carry-chair, coughing and spluttering, and wrapping his long beard around his face to keep the smoke out. No-one had thought to give Biblos a lift.

Muncle and Snarg flew down through the ash cloud – and nearly crashed into another dragon and its passenger about to take off.

Titan Bulge.

The two dragons skidded to a halt.

'Help me,' Biblos croaked feebly. 'Please help me, someone.'

'Take him, Titan!' Muncle cried. 'I still need to check that everyone else has gone.'

I'm not taking orders from you,' snarled Titan. His uniform was charred and half his face was badly grazed from his fall. 'I meant what I said. You're a cheat and your donkey's a fake.'

'So what healed your feet?'

'Who says they're healed? I just squeezed them into my boots so I could get into the King's Guard and fly a first-rate dragon'.

'Help me,' Biblos croaked again.

'Take him, Titan,' said Muncle, firmly. 'Take him to Back of Beyond, and do whatever he tells you. He's your Wise Man again, until I get there. '

Titan grunted. But the smoke was getting hotter and thicker and there really was no time to argue. He got off his Common Red, lifted Biblos's carry-chair and wedged it firmly between the spines on his dragon's back.

'I never thought I would fly,' said Biblos, 'but now that I must I shall try to enjoy it. You were right about the Goo after all, Muncle. I'm so sorry I didn't believe you. Aren't you coming with us?'

'Soon,' said Muncle. 'Very soon.'

He watched to make sure Titan headed off in the right direction. They were only just in time.

Now things started to happen fast. Shops flew into the air and came down again as a shower of rocks. The school collapsed into the seething Goo in the Crater. Last of all, the museum teetered for a moment and then crashed down the mountain towards the forest and the Smalling town.

The heat and smoke above the Crater were unbearable now. Muncle flew Snarg out of the ash cloud and round in a wider circle for one last look at the mountain that had been his home all his life.

From the north side the mountain looked much as it had always done, but the south side – the south side had simply *gone*. There was just a massive hole like a new Crater, spewing rivers of Goo towards the Smalling town. Muncle could see the lights of Smalling

carts streaming away into the distance. He turned Snarg north. But the dragon, for the first time, refused to obey. He turned south, towards the Smalling town.

'Whoa, Snarg, what are you doing? NO!'

Snarg was plunging towards the ground.

'No, Snarg, no! The Smalling town's on fire!'

He blew 'Stop' and 'Up' but Snarg took no notice. And then Muncle saw what the dragon had seen. A tiny figure with yellow hair, cut off from the Smalling town by a river of boiling Goo. Emily!

Snarg swooped down, snatched Emily in his claws and flew up again. Muncle could hear Emily shrieking. But where could they go now? The ash cloud was sweeping towards them and hiding their view of anywhere that might be safe to land.

'Pull your shirt over your face, Emily!' Muncle yelled, wrapping his jerkin over his own nose and mouth. 'Shut your eyes and try to hold your breath.'

Coughing and spluttering, Snarg somehow found his way to the other side of the mountain. He lowered Emily gently to the ground and then landed so that she could get on board properly.

'Oh, *thank* you, Muncle.' Emily coughed tearfully as she pulled her shirt away from her sooty face. '*Thank* you.'

'Don't thank *me*, it was Snarg who found you. I don't know how he managed to see you through all the smoke.'

'He didn't see me.' Emily was still spluttering and gasping for breath. 'He *heard* me.' She waved his old school dragon flute.

'Flimflams! I'm surprised he could hear that over the noise Mount Grumble is making. *I* certainly didn't.'

'Dragons must be able to hear different sounds from giants. My grandma's dog can hear sounds that we can't.'

The shrill notes that had upset the dragons earlier rang out again. Snarg yelped and a puff of smoke came out of his ears. Emily snatched the magic box out of her bag.

'It's all right, Mum,' she said, struggling not to cough. 'I'm still safe. Don't worry. I'll follow you. I've got a lift from a friend.' She looked at Muncle. 'Yes, a very, very good friend.'

She put the thing back in her bag. 'They've left,' she said, choking back tears. 'The police *made* them leave.

They're driving to Grandma's.' She looked at Muncle, her blue eyes full of worry. 'I've got to get there on my own. Can you take me?'

Now it was time for Muncle to return all the favours that Emily had done for him. He looked at the last of the giants and dragons disappearing towards the horizon.

'How far away is your grandma's?'

'Two hours by car, a bit less on the train. But I can't go by train, I haven't got any money.'

Muncle had no idea what a train was. But he understood only too well that Emily had no way of getting to her grandma's without his help.

'You don't need money to travel on Snarg,' he said bravely. 'Where does your grandma live?'

'Oh, Muncle, thank you thank you thank you. She lives at the coast.'

'What's that?'

'It's where the land stops and the sea begins.'

Muncle was horrified. 'But Sea is just a myth, Emily,' he said. 'When you get to the end of the land you just drop off the edge. Sea doesn't exist.'

'Of course the sea exists. I go there every Christmas and summer. I learned to swim in the sea, and Dad has a little boat he sails on it.'

Muncle had no answer to that. She'd been right about the volcano. All he could do was hope she was right about Sea too. He swallowed the lump of fear in his throat. 'So how do we get there?' he said.

'Follow that river. There, look. It goes all the way to the sea.' She pointed. Below them a ribbon of water glinted in the moonlight.

The river was heading south. Muncle turned for one last lingering look at the North Star. Below it there was nothing but more stars. The last dragons were already out of sight. He would have to make the flight to Back of Beyond on his own. But not yet.

He turned back. 'All right,' he said. 'Let's go.'

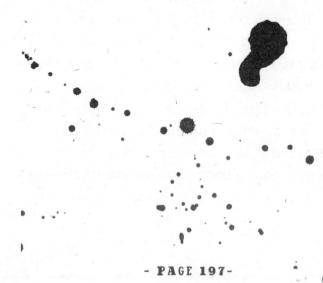

Chapter twenty

They followed the river for a long, long time. Several times Muncle had to hold on to Emily because she fell asleep, but she always jerked awake again. He was tired too, and hoped he wouldn't fall asleep himself. And what about Snarg? If *he* got tired, out here in the middle of Smalling country, it would be a disaster.

But Snarg flew on strongly. The river flowed through small and large towns and a row of low hills. Then it got wider, twisting like a snake across flatter country.

'Look!' Emily suddenly pointed into the distance. 'We've done it – there's the sea.'

Far ahead a narrow strip along the horizon shimmered in the moonlight. Gradually it grew wider and became a field of silver – it wasn't a bit how

Muncle had imagined Sea from the legends. And then they were over another town.

'This is it!' said Emily excitedly. 'There's the pier, look, that thing like a bridge sticking out into the sea. Turn left, Muncle. Grandma's street is there! It's that one, with the church on the corner. We must find somewhere to land.'

'There's only the road. Nowhere else is wide enough.'

They looked all round. The street was empty. All but one of the houses were in darkness.

'I'll risk it. Be ready to jump off quick if someone comes.'

Muncle blew 'Land' very softly and they glided down on to the road.

'Oh, there's our car. They're here, Muncle. Mum and Dad are here!'

Emily jumped down excitedly. Muncle jumped down after her for a goodbye hug. He remembered to make it a gentle one.

'Thank you so much, Muncle. If you could stay here for ever I wouldn't have time to say thank you enough. You saved my life.'

'Emily, you *risked* your life to save us. I should be

thanking you.'

At the house with a light on, a door opened and a Smalling came out. He was about Muncle's height and was wearing a sort of coat tied loosely over some light striped trousers.

'Dad!' cried Emily, and she ran up to the Smalling and flung her arms round him.

'Emily! Oh, Emily, thank God you're safe!'

A woman rushed out of the door. She had the same yellow hair as Emily and was wearing a flimsy dress that reached to her ankles. Her feet were as bare as Muncle's.

'Mum!' shouted Emily.

'Oh, darling,' gasped the woman. 'Thank heavens – we've been worried sick. I've been trying to phone you all night but your battery must be flat. So who's this friend who gave you a lift? I didn't hear a car.'

Emily's parents looked up and down the street. It was lit by a bright torch on a pole but the shadows it cast were nowhere near big enough to hide Muncle and Snarg.

'What on earth is that?' Emily's ma whispered.

'It's all right, Mum. Dragons aren't a bit how you think. Snarg looks fierce but he's really kind and helpful. He belongs to my friend Muncle.'

Muncle hadn't been this close to a Smalling since two men with sticks had chased him into the forest when he'd tried to visit Emily's town. But it would be rude not to say hello. Slowly he walked over to Emily's parents.

Emily's ma shrieked and hid behind her husband.

'Tell me I'm dreaming,' muttered her pa, rubbing his eyes with his fists. 'Tell me I'll wake up in the morning in my own bed.'

'No, Dad,' Emily said gently. 'This isn't a nightmare. Snarg really is a dragon. And Muncle really is a giant – he just happens to be a small one. And he saved my life.'

'How do,' said Muncle, nervously holding out a grey, warty hand.

Emily's pa took a deep breath, and very, very carefully shook Muncle's hand. 'We can't thank you enough, Mr ...'

Emily giggled. 'You don't have to call him mister, Dad. Muncle's my age.'

'Really? Then you've done remarkably well, young man, remarkably well.'

Emily gave Muncle another hug. 'Thanks again, Muncle,' she said, 'Have a safe journey.'

Emily stood at the gate to watch them take off, her

parents' arms around her. She waved and waved, and Muncle waved back until he could no longer see her. Then he looked up at the sky. It was still dark enough for him to see the North Star.

'Come on, Snarg,' he said. 'Emily's with her ma and pa, and we've got to find mine now. She proved us wrong about volcanoes and Sea, but now it's our turn to prove Emily wrong about Back of Beyond. It's time to go and find the place where dragons and giants truly belong.'

Snarg gave an indignant snort and puffed out a string of smoke rings.

'You're quite right,' Muncle said. 'The place where Wonder Donkeys belong too.'

THE END

Acknowledgements

JANET FOXLEY
Very many thanks to Imogen Cooper and Rachel Leyshon, who
between them found this story lurking among a confusion of sub-plots.

A big thank you also to the rest of The Chicken House team who open
the post, sell the foreign rights, and carry out all those unseen but
indispensable tasks in between.

Last – but certainly not *least* – a **HUGE** thank you to the giants of
Mount Grumble for not eating me on my frequent research visits.
I would like to think this is because I've attained the status of Trusted
Smalling, but fear it may have more to do with my looking old
and tough.

STEVE WELLS
Hi Ned, this one's for you. Thanks for lending me the rocks.